CASHAY

CASHAY

by Margaret McMullan

HOUGHTON MIFFLIN

Houghton Mifflin Harcourt
Boston New York 2009

CASHAY

Copyright © 2009 by Margaret McMullan

Houghton Mifflin is an imprint of Houghton Mifflin Harcourt Publishing Company.

www.hmhbooks.com

The text of this book is set in Garth Graphic.
Illustrations by Richard Tuschman
Design by Sheila Smallwood

Library of Congress Cataloging-in-Publication Data
McMullan, Margaret.
  Cashay / by Margaret McMullan.
      p. cm.
  Summary: When her world is turned upside down at her sister's death,
a mentor is assigned to fourteen-year-old Cashay to help her through her anger and grief.
  ISBN 978-0-547-07656-0
  [1. Grief—Fiction. 2. Anger—Fiction. 3. Mentoring—Fiction. 4. Racially mixed people—Fiction.]
I. Title.

PZ7.M4787923Cas 2009
[Fic]—dc22

                                2008036111

Manufactured in the United States of America
QUM 10 9 8 7 6 5 4 3 2 1

For my sister, Carlette

CHAPTER 1

We walk the same speed. Everything's in time. Today I have my hair pulled back in a fluffy ponytail, and Sashay has hers in two twists tied and decorated with red beads that bang into her face, brushing her lips as she talks. One hour ago she was talking in her cartoon voice, saying, "I like bread and jam!" And "The sky is so bluesy-woesy!" and it was driving me crazy.

We're not like the other Chicago girls our age living in Cabrini Green. We don't paint our nails purple or wear strawberry lip gloss or mess with our clothes like they do. Maybe because we can't. Maybe because we don't want to. Maybe because we're not thinking about boys because we got each other. Still, we got the best hair in the neighborhood because our mama's always fussing with it, trying out a new weave or sewing in some new extensions.

I don't want to be almost fourteen but I am. When you're fourteen everybody starts to notice you. I want to press the pause button and then wait until the rest of me catches up.

It's October and the bulldozers are out and on, cutting up and raising rubble. We reach North Avenue and Sashay stops at the intersection even though we got the green.

"Aw, dang," she says.

"What is it?"

"I forgot to finish my homework."

"Sashay! What'd I tell you? I'll do the math, but you got to do the other stuff your own self."

"I know. I know. But it's easier if you flunk."

"I can't keep flunking, Sashay. I told you I'd do it that one time. But that's it." I am supposed to be in the eighth grade this year, but I flunked because this way I stay in school with Sashay, and year after next we'll go together to Freemont High School. I step out into the street. I'm so mad, I don't see the red light and I don't look both ways.

"Cashay! Look out!" Sashay grabs my arm and pulls me out of the way of a cab speeding right past my toes. She stares at me, then holds out her hand, which I catch, and she goes: "You crazy."

We cross the street on WALK, turn left, and we're at Jefferson.

"Give it here," I say, and Sashay smiles big, ear to ear. Even her beads have to move out of the way for all those teeth. She pulls a sheet of math problems from her backpack and hands it over.

"I'll do it in homeroom."

We pass the part of the playground where the boys play basketball. Already the woman who sits at a table playing checkers with herself is out next to the men playing dominoes. We pass the part where Big Buddha is out on the other side of the fence dealing. He's the boyfriend of our neighbor, the one who had to quit school because she got pregnant. I won't be like her. Sashay won't be like her. We don't want a mistake. Those girls—all my neighbors who get pregnant and do drugs—they just cut down their lives. Sashay and I say getting pregnant is about the worst thing that could happen to either one of us.

We don't eat breakfast but Sashay and I do just about everything else right. We try to stay out of serious trouble. Last time I got in trouble, it was because I talked back to Sashay's teacher. I said to her, *How you expect my little sister to do her homework if you don't explain it right?* What I meant was *How you expect me to do Sashay's homework if you don't explain it right?*

I'm not a pretty girl. I know, because when my mama sees a pretty girl on TV, she says, *Oh, she's a pretty girl,* and she never says that about me. Nobody calls me cute either. Sashay, she's cute. Always was, always will be. That's a fact. Sashay looks like me, except she's pretty. She's smaller than I am and smilier. She moves like her name—all smooth and wiggly at once.

I'm not black and I'm not white either. I'm some shade of colored my mama calls *café au lait.* Sashay had a different daddy, so she's full brown. I saw my daddy once. He was a light brown man with a little head who laughed a lot then went to Memphis for good. Sashay never knew her daddy. Mama says he took off, to Detroit maybe. Mama says I have my daddy's wild spirit and Sashay got her daddy's eyes. Sometimes Mama calls us her little mutts on account of our mixed blood. I've got big lips that pooch out when they're mad, OK hair, a thirty-four-inch waist, and size-nine shoes.

"He a cracker head," Sashay says, pointing to a man-boy dressed in his bad-assed baggy gangbanger clothes, buying from Big Buddha. He sees us and runs to catch up.

"Don't point, fool," I say, pushing Sashay's hand to her side. "That's T-Rex and he's trouble." His black hair is dyed yellow and it looks like fire coming up out of his head, as he crosses over and stands in our way.

"Hey, look-a-here. If it idn't Miss CashaynSashay. You see my new watch?" He flashes his gold watch and his gold chains and his gold teeth. "You could help me out, Sashay. Make a lot of money working for me."

"Oh, yeah? Doing what?" Sashay says, but I nudge her hard.

T-Rex smiles big at Sashay. "Any number of things."

"We late for school, fool," I say to T-Rex. "You remember? S-C-H-O-O-L?" I spell it out for him, then feel bad about that because I can't remember if he quit school before or after he learned to read and write.

"Why you spelling back there?" Sashay says while we go running into school. Sashay is special ed. She doesn't have the rocking, clicking, or weird thinking that most crack kids have, but Sashay is slow and I catch her banging her head against our blue wall every now and then. We got plans. I help Sashay enough to get her through eighth grade, then we'll settle down and start our real lives in high school. Sashay has a crazy list of all that she wants to be: a musician, an actress, a model, a teacher, a track athlete like Jackie Joyner-Kersee, a coach, and a pediatrician. I don't know what I want.

Inside Ms. Feeley's classroom I sit at my desk in the back and work Sashay's problems.

I'm good at math. I never need a calculator. Alls I do is look at the numbers and set my mind to figuring. It's easy for me. Sometimes when Ms. Feeley wants a smoke, she lets me teach the class. Really. How will I use my math skills? They will help me with sales. I can take 70 percent off in less than a second and I know enough to know that 10 or even 15 percent off is hardly worth my time. I always know exactly how much money I have in my pocket—one dollar and sixty-seven cents right now—and how much that will get me at the Quick Mart—two cans of chicken rice soup. Today, maybe we'll get one can of soup and some dessert. Twinkies are OK, but I like Sno Balls— the pink kind with coconut. Sashay and I like to scoop the filling out with our fingers first.

We will go to the Quick Mart before supper today. I've taught Sashay how to pay without touching: White people behind counters don't like you to put the money in their hands if you're black. They don't want to touch you. They want you to put your money on the counter and that's the way I've learned Sashay. I can understand it. I don't want to touch them none either.

I look up and I see Sashay through the window in the door. She's on the other side waving her hands, mouthing, *Homework! Homework!*

I raise my hand. Ms. Feeley wants to know what I want. Ms. Feeley's wearing her Halloween vest with sequined candy corn and glow-in-the-dark pumpkins. I tell her I got to give something to my sister, Sashay. She sees Sashay at the door, then nods for me to go on and give it to her.

"This is the last time, Sashay. I mean it," I say, handing over her homework.

She smiles, nods, then runs. I can hear her beads clickity-clacking all the way down the hall, and what can I say? I have to smile.

* * * *

After school, cheerleaders are out practicing, singing some song about breathing in and breathing out. Like we really need instructions. Next year they'll all be in high school—Freemont, most likely. They all straighten their hair and start wearing thong underwear when they go off to high school.

We pass a guy named Genesis frenching a girl named Tequila.

"Is tequila alcohol?" Sashay says, putting a piece of bubblegum in her mouth.

"Your name doesn't signify who you are," I say.

"Is that a word?" she says. "*Signify?*"

"Every word I say is a word."

Already, it smells like snow and the light is going away. T-Rex, the same gangbanger dude in the baggy clothes and fiery hair, is out there on the other side of the fence, giving it to Big Buddha, yelling and pointing his long fingers into Big Buddha's big stomach. When we get closer, I see T-Rex's gold front teeth like he trying to be Trick Daddy himself.

He's saying bad, mean, angry words. Dirty words.

We walk past. Fast.

Sashay takes out her homework, the one I did for her. "I got an A," she says. "An *A!*"

"She say anything on it?"

Sashay stops to read the teacher's note on the top of the page.

"Hurry up, Sashay." I want to get past Big Buddha and out of T-Rex's way.

"'Nice job,'" she says real slow, smiling. That's how Sashay reads.

"That's it? 'Nice job'?"

Sashay holds the paper out for me to see, and I look it over, saying, "I suppose that's better than 'OK.'"

Somebody turns up some bossy, nasty rap.

"Come on," I whisper. I don't want Sashay's or my own ears to hear this music. I don't want those words in my head. "Walk fast."

I hear men's voices all around us, sounding low and creepy, saying things nobody says. A green car speeds by, then screeches to a stop. And *Bam! Bam!* We hear a gun go off two times. A car door slams and everybody's running and screaming or going down, covering their heads with books and handbags and groceries. Sashay and I lie down on the cement the way we've been taught, our cheeks on the cold, cracked pavement. We face each other.

"Dang," I say.

"Oh, no," she says. Sashay looks real scared.

"What?"

"I swallowed my gum."

I lift my head and look back. I don't see T-Rex anywhere.

"Somebody shot Big Buddha," I say.

"That gum will clog up my insides," Sashay says.

"What are you talking about?"

"Don't be mad," Sashay says.

People all around us begin to stand up and look around. Everything's too quiet. I'm wondering why we don't hear sirens yet.

"Come on, Sashay. We gotta get out of here."

Sashay's just lying there with her eyes open, looking at me.

"Come on, Sashay. Don't be scared." I try not to sound scared. I try to sound bored. "Come on, Sashay. We'll be late and Mama'll be worried. You know how she gets."

A line of blood the color of nail polish moves from somewhere under Sashay.

"Sashay?" I whisper. My face feels sweaty and my eyes sting.

Sashay closes her eyes. I move close to her, quick, my elbows on the cement. Behind her I see the pool of blood puddling. I put my head down next to hers. We're face to face, like two spoons on their sides.

"Talk to me, sister," I scream into her candy-smelling coat.

Sashay's eyes open. "There you go," I say, sounding like Mama, taking both her hands in mine. "Breathe in. Breathe out. Don't you go nowhere without me, Sashay. Help is coming."

She looks at me scared and she wants to say something. Her eyes, they say, *Oh God!* and *What is this pain?* to me, then they open big and close again and open looking different, like they seen something somewhere inside her head that they like and can't say no to. Then they close and I can't smell her breath.

I wait for sirens. I wait for the earth to stop moving. I wait for everything to come to an end, but the worst happens. Nothing. Sashay does not breathe. The sirens do not come. The earth does not stop moving. I look up, and in lit-up windows all around, I see people—just their heads—like pumpkins looking down at us, not smiling, not frowning, just watching. On the street, people who don't see us talk and walk and that doesn't seem right at all to me. People who do see us begin to gather around and ask if we're OK.

The sky goes from gray to brown to black.

We are not OK.

Nothing is right at all anymore.

There is no more Sashay. It's like nothing.

And then, then I hear the sirens.

CHAPTER 2

I'm not tender-headed, but when Mama cornrows she can braid the brains out of your head no matter how much she greases you up. I don't need my head hurting any more right now, so the night before we bury Sashay, I tell Mama to lock me up.

Mama never cared for dreadlocks. She says they look too ethnic, whatever that means. But right now, Mama doesn't seem to mind. She uses Murray's because she gets it free from the salon and it smells nice and it's way better than petroleum jelly. Some people use beeswax, but it can start smelling funky after a while. My hair is between straight and kinky and it doesn't take a ton of grease to untangle. She twists and twists and the pulling and yanking feels about right.

We don't talk. When she found out, Mama cried cried cried. Now she doesn't talk hardly at all.

* * * *

Mama spends all our saved-up money on clothes, shoes, and a white coffin. The first time I ever wear black is to Sashay's funeral. Sashay wears white.

In the church there are people I know but don't recognize, their faces different because they aren't smiling. My Aunt Jo'Neisha sits by me and holds me tight to her while Mama sits staring down at her hands. I don't hear what the preacher or anybody else says. I hold the shoebox full of Sashay's cicada shell collection. Before we left for the funeral, I tried to hunt down what Sashay liked. She liked a poem that she wrote once on a scrap of paper: *The smile blooms teeth. The apple readies to run.* I put that in the shoebox. She liked sinking her hand into a bowl full of dried beans. She liked loading Mama's leftover cold coffee with sugar then slurping it down slow. She liked wearing my old sweatshirts that smelled like Sashay and me both, smelling the way we laughed together on good days. She liked the stink of gas at gas stations and she liked how the lids open and close on Tic Tac boxes. She liked cicadas.

I know that the dead Sashay is supposed to look like she's just sleeping, but when I pass her and see her laid out inside her white box, wearing her white dress and her white patent leather shoes, I know that it is not Sashay. It is dead Sashay, so I don't cry, and I hear people whisper about me—how they think I'm in shock or I am cold and unfeeling, how I might be strange.

We ride out to the cemetery in a long white car that cost too much money, and my Aunt Jo'Neisha is telling my mama how we need to be sure that they put the right body into the right hole with the right marker, how you can never be too sure about crooked under-takers. Aunt Jo'Neisha works as a maid at a hospital and she knows about these things.

I think that Sashay's shoebox full of cicadas should go with her, but at the last minute, as we watch her little white coffin get lowered into the ground, I decide to keep them myself. I can't go over to the edge of that hole and give them back to Sashay. I tell her, "I need them now, if that's OK with you." And it's like now they're more than a box full of ugly old bug skeletons.

Back at our apartment, I sit alone on my side of the bed, looking over at Sashay's side. Once, from her side of the bed, she said to me, "I just want to hug your toes." And I told her she was crazy. Now I wish I hadn't.

I'm still in my black dress and my new black shoes. Before, Mama wouldn't allow us to wear black. She said it was a woman's color. I guess I became a woman when Sashay got shot. The shoes hurt my feet and make me feel all crumbly. I tap them together, scuffing the shine on purpose. Outside my door, Mama is on the couch with Aunt Jo'Neisha, crying crying crying. I do not want to have my feelings right there in front of everyone to see. I've got crying in me, but I don't know when it's going to come out. So I stay here, on this bed, in my room. On the window ledge is the box full of coupons and two-for-one deals Sashay and I kept. Somebody came over with a ham. I can smell the pink meat. I look out the window at mostly sky, brick, and bulldozers and I don't see anything.

Aunt Jo'Neisha taps on my door. "You all right?" she says.

I just stare at her. Aunt Jo'Neisha's not fat, but

she's big, and she's always wearing a skirt and a blouse because she's always getting ready to go to work. She's not pretty, but her eyes smile even when she doesn't.

She comes and sits down on the bed, on Sashay's side. She puts her arm around me and we set to rocking. Aunt Jo'Neisha is Mama's older sister. A long time ago, she talked about going to school to become some kind of a nurse. Now she just works.

"We thought about being dead, Sashay and me," I whisper. "But we never thought about getting killed."

"Worst that could happen and you not even sixteen," Aunt Jo'Neisha says, shaking her head, rocking, and saying *umn umn umn.* "When you hurt like this, just hold on, and one day the pain will go away."

We keep rocking. I hold on.

"Now I know what to be scared of," I say. "That's something."

* * * *

For days, people keep coming in and out of our apartment and I don't know them. They bring food over. More food than I've ever seen, but we don't eat much of it. I eat differently now. I chew more and when I swallow I can't feel the food going down and I can't taste. Sometimes I get too worn out what with all the chewing and I just quit and spit it out. Still, I smell it all—the noodle casseroles, the baked beans, the corn bread. Instead of eating, Mama and I mostly smell dinners.

One night, the night the weather changes from cold to colder, I wake up smelling hot dogs. I go out into the living room, where Mama sleeps on the couch. It's cold and smoky and the window is open. I can see my breath coming out in thick clouds.

"Mama? Why you eatin' hot dogs without me?"

I hear a man giggle. I never heard a man giggle before. Men laugh. Little boys giggle. "You hear that?" this man says. "She think we eatin' hot dogs. She think my weed smells like hot dogs." He can't quit giggling.

"Baby. Go back to bed," Mama says.

I take one last look at them there on the sofa.

Mama's a mess. It's like she has turned into another person. She hasn't slept and she hasn't changed and her hair's all wacky. Even her skin has gone all blotchy black. She needs to go back to work. She's leaning into Mr. Giggles like she's needing something.

It used to be that I wondered who exactly my daddy was, but worrying about daddies now is way back there in my mind. Now? Sashay stands on the front balcony of my brain, waving at me when I wake up and when I go to sleep. She won't leave me alone. She jumps out there sometimes, shouting out at me from that concrete ledge.

I leave them be. I go back to my room, back to my side of the bed, careful not to mess up Sashay's side. If a dog lived anywhere near us, I would have heard it barking now, outside my window. I hear a buckle noise coming from Mama's room.

Once upon a time Mama painted one wall in this room blue because that's all the paint we could pay for. I face this blue wall and I stare at it. Sashay and I used to joke about training a cockroach to be our pet, using dental floss for a leash. You don't see pets around my neighborhood. You don't hear dogs barking; you hear jackhammers and the El every now and then. Maybe a siren. I keep staring at the wall, thinking up pet cockroach names, and I fall into some kind of sleep.

* * * *

The bulldozers are out screaming early in the morning, but still nothing, not even the racket, wakes up Mama. They've torn down all but a few of the buildings because they're putting up something called Something-Something Village. Like calling the projects a village now is going to change everything.

I look in at Mama. She's all flopped out in the pull-out sofa, asleep with him, with Mr. Giggles. They don't move, his arm weighed down on her back. He's a narrow black man with tiny ears and long fingers with white cracks in his knuckles. And there's Mama with her see-through hair. Mama's hair started falling out the day we buried Sashay.

Before, she'd be up, dressed in her work clothes, telling us to drink some orange juice. Before, she'd be stuffing things in her purse, getting her food stamps together to go shopping after work, checking herself in the mirror. Before. Back when Sashay was not dead Sashay. Back when we thought getting pregnant was the worst thing that could happen to us—that and getting bit by a West Nile mosquito.

Mama has already taken two weeks off work, and I don't know how that beauty salon will take to her taking another.

"Mama? You gon' be late for work," I say.

Mama moves her head. She doesn't open her eyes, like she can't open them. "Go away," she says. "My bones hurt."

* * * *

The cold is cold now. On Thanksgiving I open three cans of chili for Mr. Giggles, Mama, and me. In the early morning, outside, the air goes right through my pants and socks. You have to respect that.

Sometimes Sashay walks with me to and from school. Sometimes she's drinking orange juice. Sometimes she rides a bike. A shiny red one. I know my mind is playing tricks, but where did she get a bike? Where did she get all that energy when she's supposed to be dead?

In school I know how to be there and not be there. I know how to sit up straight, do my work, and not listen to boys because they never say anything important. I do what my teacher says to do. Ms. Feeley, she's talking to us about violent motion.

"How does an arrow keep going when you shoot it from a bow?" she asks.

I'm thinking, *How could I have stopped that bullet from going into Sashay? Why didn't it miss her and go into me? And who the hell invented guns anyway? And what would the projects be like if there were bows and arrows instead? And why does motion* have *to be violent?*

I heard once that when you get shot, it burns. It feels like you're burning. Did Sashay feel she was on fire when she lay there, staring?

For weeks then months I keep at it. I do my work. Everything outside stands still and freezes. I don't remember what the weather does exactly because I forget how to feel. I try to figure out the atom, matter, and poetry that doesn't rhyme. I listen and twist my hair with my fingers, relieved that at least I'm not tender-headed or pretty.

You're not supposed to wash your hair for six months when you have dreadlocks. The more water you use on your hair, the slower your hair takes to lock. In all it only takes me three months to lock up.

CHAPTER 3

Mama screaming wakes me up. She's calling out, "Cashay! Cashay! Come get these boys off the ceiling." In the living room the TV is on with the sound off. Mama's under the covers alone. I look up at the ceiling.

"Mama. There ain't nothing on the ceiling."

She pokes her head out. Her eyes are puffy and I can barely make out the dark part in the center. Mr. Giggles was over again last night but he's not here now, thank God. He's got her on a pipe now. He's got her looking like a Halloween skeleton.

"Right up there?" she says. "See?" She's looking

all over the ceiling at nothing. She needs her hair cut and fixed. She is wearing the same clothes she had on last week.

I shake my head.

"Call work for me, will you? Say I can't come in. Tell 'em I'm sick. I am. I'm sick." She goes back under the covers.

"Mama. There's no one left to call. You done lost your job two months ago."

"I got to do Miss Martinez today," Mama says under the covers. "Second Tuesday of the month. Lovely dark curls."

Mama tells anyone who asks that she's in her period of bereavement. That's what she calls this crazy state she's in: bereavement. She stays home watching TV, smoking whatever Mr. Giggles brings over, and then she sends me out for cheesy Doritos when she gets hungry.

I open her purse for money. Nothing but a few food stamps. I go out, and with the food stamps I buy Lucky Charms, hot dogs, Velveeta, buns, and a kind of soda that's cheap. I bring it back home, eat some, and leave the rest for Mama.

* * * *

I go to a school where every grade is a different color locker. Seventh is blue. I am blue. I wish I were back in sixth, when I was yellow.

I eat lunch for free at school and I put leftovers and anything extra I find in my coat pockets. I never take off my coat. A girl sits down at lunch with me. She was in Sashay's class. Sashay liked this girl. She liked touching her huge, weird hair. This girl doesn't say anything to me. I know she wants to be friends, but I don't want friends. She watches me while she eats.

"What you looking at?" I say. My locks are thick and snaky and hang down to my shoulders. Sometimes my hair scares people and that's just fine by me. My eyes tell this girl to get up and leave and she does.

* * * *

We're reading stupid books—books about white people who lose pets. We're reading about where the red fern grows and I don't know what a red fern is and I don't care either.

It's Valentine's Day and I forgot. Everybody's wearing red, passing out stupid cards and little hearts with stupid words like "Kiss Me." Ms. Feeley puts us into twos—reading partners. When I read, the words don't come out right. The edges bump into my teeth and get stuck on my tongue. This kid, Jeremiah, makes fun of me, calls me a bucket head. I don't even bother to stand up when I hit him hard in the face.

When we do stand up, we're at each other. How am I to know how strong I am? I've never been what they call petite. I'm a big girl. And I know how to use my legs and my weight. I don't see the window but I hear the glass crack when his head smacks into it. Still, it's *his* fault. He shouldn't have made fun of me and he shouldn't have fallen against the window when I shoved him.

There's a lot of shouting and everyone's standing around us. Somebody's pulling me off Jeremiah. It's Ms. Feeley. I think of what that singer Trina says in one song and I say it to Ms. Feeley. It is so nasty, everybody stops shouting and there is quiet. I don't know why I say this, I just do. I think that I have rights now because of what happened to Sashay.

* * * *

The principal's office is quiet and I think I could just sit here for a while and stare out a window, but the principal comes in. He's in a suit with a Winnie-the-Pooh tie and he tells me this is Valentine's Day, a day about love, not hate. He introduces me to a counselor lady who's wearing black ankle boots and a red skirt, and she sits down in a chair next to mine.

"It was stupid," I say. "What I should have done was just yank his hair and sit on him, but I didn't think of it in time."

"Is that what you really think? That's the only thing you regret?"

I look at that woman straight on. "Yeah. That's what I regret."

"Look. I know you're angry," she starts. "I just want to find out how angry." She gives me a sheet of paper and tells me to write down the answers to the questions.

The questions all start out the same. Someone treats me unfairly. Someone is being rude or annoying. Someone starts a fight. The question is how would I react? I write in that I'm usually the someone in the question. The last question has to do with hearing news about a terrorist attack, like the one that happened that year in New York on September 11. I just write down that I live in a war zone and I already been attacked by a terrorist and he's still living in the hood.

This woman, this white woman counselor, she wears rings on her thumbs and she's peeling an orange. I give her the paper and she gives me half the orange, already peeled. I hold it in my hand. Fresh fruit, raw in my fingers.

She looks over the paper. "How old are you now, Cashay?" She's eating the orange. I'm not.

"Twelve," I lie. "What difference does it make?"

"You're almost fourteen. You'd be starting high school next year if you had wanted to. What do you want to do with your life?"

I can't think about the future. Sometimes I can think about the past. Mostly, I can think about now and how I'm going to make my way through it.

"I hate that word, *life*," I say.

"You're not thinking of suicide, are you?"

"Why would I be thinking about that?"

She leans back in her plastic leather chair, looking way too relieved.

And then I lose it. I have to stand up and walk around the room. She doesn't look scared so I don't feel like breaking anything. I tell her Sashay didn't just die. She was killed. She was shot. She was twelve years old and she was walking home from school and she was murdered. Everybody acts like that's natural, like it's bound to happen.

"Why? Huh? Why is that OK? Because she was black? Because she was just a kid? Because she was

[28]

living where she was living? And that bad-ass who shot her? He's out there walking around, free, and he's a killer. That natural? That a part of *life?* When did *life* get so messed up anyway?"

She's just watching me, letting me have it all out. Then she says, "You know who killed Sashay? Did you tell the police?"

I stare at a pencil on the desk. I look at the orange sections, all mashed up in my hand. I don't know how or when I smashed the orange. I wish I hadn't. I wish I could eat a whole orange now, then go get a Big Mac and two pink Sno Balls. I want a treat. I want to sleep for a long time, like a year.

I hear her pick up the phone, ask for some police station.

* * * *

Sure I know them. I know all them. Everybody knows everybody in the projects but sometimes you pretend like you don't. T-Rex? He's in that gang. There's just the three of them—three punks trying to get in with the big boys, riding around in that stupid green car. They'd kill me if they knew I was even thinking that, but that's the truth. They're out there hanging, all duded up in baggy clothes, their pants riding low. They hold on to their crotches like something down there's going to fall off. They need their drugs and their guns to feel like men. The one who looks most like a girl? The one with the gold front tooth? That's the one who shot Sashay. T-Rex. Like the dinosaur with an above-room-temperature IQ. He shot Big Buddha too. But I hate hate hate them all.

This is what I tell the police when the white counselor takes me down to the station. It was not new to me to see wreckage, but I never been to the police before, usually walk the other way, never into their building. It's all hallways and doors and overhead lights that buzz. And it smells like piss and floor wax. The white people look at me, noticing me, probably hating me, but I don't care.

I hate T-Rex. I hate Mama and Mr. Giggles. I want to be dead. Dead with Sashay.

Afterward, after I tell them all that I know, they give me a Happy Meal.

* * * *

The air is so cold my nostrils freeze together when I breathe walking home. I bite into the coldness. Mama is gone. I try smoking what I seen Mama and Mr. Giggles smoke. I sit down, light the little leftover, twisted cigarette, but I can't hold that bad-tasting smoke in my mouth, and I cough, spitting it out, and my tongue feels like it's burning and the burning scares me, and it feels like I think a bullet might feel and I think, *Why do I want to do myself this way?* I didn't even know it until now, but I felt just fine before. Now my chest hurts because I'm messing with myself. So I put that little twisted cigarette out and flush it down the toilet, and think, *Well, that sure didn't do me any good.*

There's nothing for dinner and still no Mama. I find a sack of groceries with bread and cans of soup near the door. There's a note inside that says "Take care, love, Jo'Neisha." I fix myself a peanut butter and jelly sandwich and eat it. Then I start to heat up a can of soup. I look around. The couch is all stained with orange marks from all the Cheetos and Doritos Mama eats.

Sashay sucked her thumb. When she turned ten she only sucked it at night so no one would make fun of her. It didn't bother me none, and she knew that. Now I'm glad I never fussed after her about it. I like to think that Sashay's sitting on a cloud, sucking that thumb of hers as much as she likes.

I hurry, take the soup off the burner, and eat it

cold. I fix myself another sandwich and eat that. And then one more. I brush my teeth and change quick into my pajamas so I can go to sleep and in my dreams maybe meet up with Sashay.

* * * *

I see the white woman counselor again. I don't want to learn her name because I don't want to be seeing her.

"You're not saying much today," she says. She's wearing a peach-colored T-shirt and she smells like rice pudding. She's got her shoes off and she's sitting cross-legged. It's the end of February in Chicago and this white woman's got her shoes off. She has three toe rings and she doesn't play with the rings the way I would have if I wore toe rings. She's got an apple too. She's peeling the apple with a knife and cutting it up into skinny little sections. She offers me a section and I say no thanks.

"Do you have any hobbies? Any interests?" she asks me.

"What, like collecting stamps?"

"Think about developing some interests, Cashay. Keeps your mind active. Your mind has a life just like your body. Both need exercising."

I'm looking at her peeling her fruit with her shoes off and I'm thinking, *Lady, you been taking too many yoga classes.*

"Just tell me what to do and I'll do it. How do I act? Tell me that. People get all quiet around me like I'm gonna break."

"They're just trying to be nice, Cashay."

"I know and I hate them for that."

"Cashay. I know you're angry."

"I'M NOT ANGRY!"

We let the air around us take in my shout and settle down until it's quiet again. Then she tells me about some afterschool program at some place with nuns.

"I don't want to be no nun."

"The nuns just run the program. It's Catholic."

"I don't know nothin' about Catholics. I'm Christian."

"Catholics are Christian, Cashay." She smiles and eats her apple. "What is it?" she says after a while, looking me over.

"I'm just wondering."

"Yes?" she says. "Go on."

I look at her desk all messed up with papers and old coffee cups. I look at her wall and wonder why she has no window. I look up at the yellow-brown water stains on the ceiling and wonder where the leaks are. "When will this all go away?"

She sighs. She sighs like a man. "It takes time. That's all."

CHAPTER
4

Aunt Jo'Neisha stands under the bald basketball hoop out there on the playground near the bulldozers, getting interviewed for the six o'clock news. She's saying, "Yeah, we have a lot of gangs. And yeah, we have a lot of drugs, but it's still home."

The black news lady goes on, giving a brief history of Cabrini Green, saying how it was first built on something the Italians lived in called Little Hell. Meanwhile, the TV cameras pan to the woman playing checkers by herself and the men playing dominoes, as if they are a sad and sorry sight, which is wrong. They are perfectly happy doing what they are doing.

They're having trouble tearing down the second to the last building, and the workmen look like cavemen trying to pull down the last woolly mammoth. They have to make it so all those bricks and mortar fall down safely, because they say the people who live here are still living even though it doesn't feel like it to me.

I sit on a park bench, and in my mind Sashay is there too, in front of the chain-link fence, and we're both trying not to breathe in the air that's full up with concrete dust. I think of Sashay, warm and cherry-smelling, humming some jump rope song. Nobody jumps a rope like Sashay. This is where Sashay and I used to fight each other with swords made out of tinfoil, fencing the way I read about somewhere, poking each other over and over. This is where we chalked all over the playground too, drawing and coloring our own private neighborhood. Over there, near where Aunt Jo'Neisha is talking to the reporter, that's where my cousin Louisa got cut. And right behind me, that's where Sashay got shot. This used to be where we played. Now this will always be the corner where Sashay got shot.

A girl from my class named Maryam sits down on the bench with us. She spells her name with an *m* at the beginning and at the end. To even it out, she says. Maryam is drinking a can of beer. "Good thing I had the baby 'cause now I can drink again."

"Move over," I say. "You're squishing us."

Maryam burps. "'Us'?" She shakes her head. "You crazy, girl," she says, then gets up and leaves.

I throw a rock at a squirrel to watch it run.

I am down here because I don't want to be up in the apartment where Mama is making out with Mr. Giggles. I come and sit on this bench in this park and dare bullets to come my way. On a good day, when the sky is bright blue and the sun is out, I close my eyes and my face warms up and I think about the bright white behind my eyelids even though my eyes are still shut. I think of what Sashay would say if she were still alive. I think about what I might say to her. "Ever seen the blue eyelids of a pigeon? You can only see them when the pigeon's dead. It's a real pretty color."

Then I open my eyes and listen to the black news lady tell me my future.

There's a lottery to get into the Something-Something Village, which everyone's just calling the Village, the nice new buildings across the street where there's a Starbucks and a Blockbuster and even a brand-new school called Benson's. We live just a mile away from Chicago's ritziest strip called the Gold Coast. Our buildings are all used up and folks are seeing a need to do away with them all—like they're a bad math formula somebody needs to erase from the board.

Only seventy-nine families from the projects can get into the Village and maybe live next door to someone who bought the same place for something around $500,000. I don't know how I'd feel if I was that family who spent $500,000, living next door to someone else who got the place for next to nothing, but I know how I feel now, and I follow Aunt Jo'Neisha, who I see heading toward the sales trailer where there's an office to sign up to get into the Village.

Aunt Jo'Neisha says she's just curious, and I can tell she might be embarrassed having said what she said to the reporter, that she's happy here because it's home. But even this sales trailer is nicer than some of the homes I've seen here.

The black woman behind the desk tells us the rules of the Village: no drugs, no loitering, no loud music. "You've got to keep regular appointments with our staff and submit to drug tests if you have a drug history or a criminal history. And you've got to be truthful about how many people are going to live there," she says.

Jo'Neisha nods. I tell the woman Jo'Neisha is my aunt, not my mama. The woman says everyone has to pass a preliminary screening process. There's a home inspection, a criminal background check, and, if you have a drug history or criminal history, there's the first mandatory drug test.

"Do you or your mama have a drug or a criminal history?"

"I don't," Aunt Jo'Neisha says. I just look at her. She wears her hair pulled back in a loose bun like she always does. I can tell now she wants in this nice new place just like me. She reminds me of me, but I don't tell her that.

I think of the social worker a few years back telling me that if Mama got into trouble again with drugs and the law, they'd send her off to some prison clinic and Sashay and I would be put into foster care. I've heard about foster care and group homes and I don't want any part of that. I can take care of Mama and me both if I have to.

"My mama's had some trouble," I say. "But that was a while ago. What do you mean, 'mandatory'?"

She tells me what I already know. Everybody has to pee into little cups and hand the cups over.

"OK," I say, like this is what we do every day. "May we please see the blueprints?" Both the woman and

Aunt Jo'Neisha look at me all surprised, like they can't believe I know the word *blueprints,* but the woman goes and gets them and spreads the sheet out on her desk and we look at them, and I can't help but smile when I see all the straight blue lines, the geometric rooms, the neat kitchens and doorways and hallways, the evenly spaced windows. The woman digs in and tells me about the budget reports and the projected costs. She points out the emergency exits and the balconies where a person can stand with a cup of hot something in the morning. Aunt Jo'Neisha leans on the counter to get a better look. I know that we both can see ourselves living here, inside these neat blue lines on this woman's desk. Here is where our lives would be different and better.

* * * *

"Mama? You gotta pee in this here cup." I give her the cup the woman gave me.

Mr. Giggles is gone and Mama doesn't even ask why I need her to do what I want her to do. She just gets up off the sofa, her eyes still watching the TV. She leaves the room with the cup, then comes back and gives it to me full.

She looks at me, the cup between us.

"You have pimples," she says, her eyes all glazed over. "Pee gets rid of pimples."

"Mama, you gone altogether crazy," I laugh.

My face feels like it's breaking when we both laugh. When did we last laugh? I want to hug Mama, but she turns away and goes and plops back down on the sofa.

"We need more money, Mama."

She doesn't answer. I take the last of the food stamps from the box in the kitchen I keep now for such things.

Mama always did go back and forth on the drugs. One time she got high, when Sashay was still alive, she cooked up a plan to go out into the country to find a field of purple hull peas. She had in mind to pick and shell all the peas a car could hold, then bring them back to the city to sell on the streets, as though purple hull peas were the drugs people were really looking for, not crack. She loved eating purple hull peas so much, she figured everyone else would too. I told her we didn't even have a car. Even after she came down from that high, she kept hold of this big money plan. This was back when the drugs hadn't taken over, back when Sashay and I would roll her leftover change and Mama always had money thoughts.

I run back down to the Village office, give the cup to the woman, and say, "I'll be in touch." She doesn't look at me funny when I say this, maybe because we've looked at the blueprints together.

* * * *

My counselor has signed me up for the afterschool program at the Catholic center with Sister Marie because she says I need to work on my homework and my anger management.

"Manage your own damn anger," I say. "I told you. I'm not even Catholic."

"And I told you. It's just *run* by the Catholics. Not everyone there is Catholic."

I tell her I hate afterschool programs where you learn to paperclip a bunch of toilet paper rolls into an ugly Christmas tree, and fifty-five-year-old women dress like six-year-olds.

"Cashay," she says, "it's March. They're done with Christmas crafts. I'll go with you the first time."

I don't see why I can't just sit for a while in her office and eat slices of fruit she peels and cuts for me. I've gotten used to this white woman. I like that she talks like she talks. I hate when grown women talk like kids and white people talk like they're black. This lady, she is goofy and she talks goofy too. A good goofy.

* * * *

When we get there, there is a multicolored sign that says CHRISTIANS UNDER CONSTRUCTION, and there are all kinds of kids, every age, and the nun, she's fifty-something and she's wearing pigtails and she tells my counselor about being "icky-sicky with a tummy ache." I shoot my counselor a look and her eyes say, *Cut it out, Cashay—don't even start.*

The room is warm and the walls are covered with finger paintings. At the end of the hall, some white men in coveralls are painting the walls—one wall blue, another red, another yellow, another green. One of the men turns around and I see that he's a she and she's smiling big, like she's trying to impress the other men, and I'm thinking, *Oh, sister, please. Quit trying so hard.*

Sister Pigtails shows us the computer room, where kids are tap-tapping away. Then she shows us a room with tables and chairs and maps all over the walls. Big people are paired with little people and they're whispering about work. I hear some worn-out grownup saying, "Well, yes, that's a good question. It's not spelled the same, but it sounds the same." A girl I know named Lowquisha is squatting underneath a rack of winter coats, holding her ears closed.

"This is our mentoring room," Sister Pigtails says. "Children from schools all around the area come and spend a few hours here every week with a mentor. The mentors come from all over too."

"How come all the grownups are white?" I ask.

Sister Pigtails shrugs and does that thing that all teachers do—she asks the question right back. "I don't know, Cashay. Why do you think that is?"

"Hell if I know." She asked for it.

Sister Pigtails wants to introduce me to my new mentor, some friend of hers named Sister Pam. This is when my counselor leaves, even though I ask her nice to please stay.

Sister Pam is dried-up skinny but she's dressed normal in a blue dress and she spends a good bit of time talking at me. It's Jesus this and Jesus that. Then she lights into me about sound money sense and the organizing principles of life while I connect the freckles that cover her face and realize that her face is made up of triangles. She goes on and on and on about hostility and anger and I try not to let it get me mad. She's saying, You need to read more. She's saying, You need to turn off the TV. She's saying, You're not one more girl on the planet who can't do math, are you?

All the nuns here are white. I never seen a black nun. If I were white and I were a nun and I sat down with kids like me, I'd be sure to brush my teeth and gargle with mint mouthwash after I drank coffee. And I would talk about stuff that mattered. I'd make us paint pictures of people and read stories about Chicago and black folks other than Martin Luther King because there is more than one black person to talk about, and when the weather got nice, I'd take the likes of me for a walk to the zoo or the beach or to that place called Grant Park.

"Are you listening to me, Cashay? Have you heard one word of what I said?"

I nod and repeat what she said.

"OK then." She seems pleased and she looks around the room at the other kids. "See that young girl over there?" she says.

I look at Juanita across the room and I have to smile. Juanita is one mean girl, fourteen going on forty, with a chest that started growing when she was two. She wants to be a social worker. She got the idea watching *Days of Our Lives.*

"Now, what do you suppose made her decide to

wear that leopard print leotard today? What kind of signal does she think she's putting out? Why would she choose to show off her breasts and not, say, her hair or her eyes?"

I look at that old flat-chested, freckle-faced triangle of a woman, Sister Pam, and she sees my eyes on her. "Because she can, lady. And I think she looks *hot.*" We have ourselves a stare down. I'm managing my anger, but my eyes are wearing army boots and they're marching.

"Well, you know, Cashay: She's never gonna make it in this world. Not with that attitude." And she smiles at me, calm and serene-like, and what I hear her say, what I know she means, is *I'm* never gonna make it in this world.

* * * *

The black woman behind the desk at the Village office shakes her head at me funny when she gives me the results of Mama's pee test.

"This *was* your mama's and not yours, right?" she says.

I nod and she tells me again what I already know— that Mama has drugs in her urine. "She has to come clean. She's gotta get off the drugs if you all want to live in the Village."

* * * *

A long time ago, before Sashay was shot, it used to be that Mama took the drugs only on Fridays. Then Thursdays, then every day, and then she couldn't get up mornings and she lost her job at the Super Save. Then one day she wanted Sashay and me to watch while she sat on the floor and ran a razorblade up and down both her arms.

After the hospital and the counseling, Mama took to Jesus, got off the drugs, earned her beautician's license and degree, and started working at the beauty salon. For three good years we were back on track, saving our monies, doing our work.

"Mama, you gotta get off them drugs." I'm standing there in front of the pullout sofa between Mama and the TV. She looks me up and down all dazed.

"I know, I know," she says. "We were just talking about that."

"Yeah? Because if you do, we got a chance. We could live across the street in those nice new buildings."

Mr. Giggles comes in right then, singing and jiggling and shaking like he's the star of his own music video and his is the only bootay worth watching. He's tall and wiry and he's got zero mojo.

Mama and I both look at him and I think she's thinking what I'm thinking.

"Baby," she says, real happy-like. "We're gonna have a baby!"

Mr. Giggles stops jiggling and singing and I stop what I'm doing and we stare at Mama and her new news.

"You jivin' me, right?"

"Mama, are you kidding?"

"No, baby. For real. I'm pregnant."

Mr. Giggles goes over and looks in the refrigerator and says something that makes me turn away. I'm thinking and thinking and not coming up with anything.

And what does he do? What does Mama do? What do they do? They plop right down, turn on the TV, and light up their pipe. There are nice-looking, comfortable rooms on the TV. The white girl on the program stops crying because the show is almost over. I'm just looking, staring, thinking there are so many people watching so much TV in so many of these rooms in these buildings in this here project. Sometimes I wonder if we're all just acting like somebody acting.

Most girls my age like babies, but like I say, I'm not most girls my age. I don't even like our neighbor kids. There are too many of them, for one. In the summer, some of them run around without clothes because they don't have air conditioning or fans. The littlest one next door ran out into the hall once, naked, playing himself like a guitar. Nobody needs to see that.

"Move your fat ass," Mr. Giggles says to me.

"Hey," Mama says, still watching the TV. "Don't talk like that to her."

"OK then," he says, giggling. "Set your flab to jigglin'."

* * * *

Sister Pam wants me to save up to buy new shoes but I don't because Mama and I have to eat. I don't tell Sister Pam the part about food. I don't tell her nothing. It's none of her business. I laugh to myself, thinking about *none* and *nun.*

Next time I see her, she's gotten me a pair of new shoes. Nike. Just the kind of shoes she figures a black girl like me would go nuts over.

"Why don't you try them on?"

"I don't want another pair of shoes."

"You *need* a new pair of shoes," she says. "Just try them. I think you'll really like them, Cashay." She's being extra nice today, but there's no way in hell I'm taking my shoes off. Not for this lady. Not for nobody.

"I don't care if you have holes in your socks," she says, and I'm thinking, *Lady, what you talking about now?*

I look at her square brown pumps. "Go buy yourself some new shoes," I say.

"Is there a problem?" Sister Pigtails can hear us. I did not know that my voice was up and out, or that my fingers were curling into fists.

"Cashay won't try on the new pair of shoes I bought her." It's like Sister Pam turned six years old and she's tattling.

"Why don't you try on the shoes, Cashay? Look at yours. You need a new pair. I mean, my goodness." Sister Pigtails is bending down now, looking at my shoes. They both are. "Is that . . . ? Could that be? Is that blood, Cashay?"

I tuck my shoes under my chair.

"Cashay?"

"Did you get into another fight at school?" Sister Pam asks.

"I wore these shoes when Sashay got shot," I say, and they both of them shut up. "The soles soaked up her blood. That's why they're brown. They used to be red but old blood is brown. You could see my footprints walking all around her body, then the footprints walked away from her. I know because I looked back and I saw."

I'm not mad anymore. I just stare and think. My favorite pair of shoes is another pair of shoes, but I do not wear those anymore. My favorite pair of shoes is a pair of blue Reeboks, but they don't remember Sashay or her dead body or the colored beads that held her dead twists. Not like my brown sneakers remember. These shoes, these tired old brown shoes, are a record.

"It's not the only thing you have left of your sister, Cashay," Sister Pam says. "You still have memories of her. Those shoes are nasty and you really should throw them out." She turns to Sister Pigtails. "I mean, there's the girl's blood still on them." She raises her voice and I think that she's fixing to grab hold of my leg. "You need to throw these shoes out, Cashay. It will be better that way."

I want to say, *Look, everybody, I tried. I tried to manage my anger.* But I finally stomp and shoot up and shout out, "Leave me be, lady." And I'm out of there. I'm out of there. My bloody brown shoes are running and they take me away to where I see a bunch of brown leaves near a fence and I bend and fill my hands up with dry leaves and I crunch crunch crunch them in my hands until I'm calmed down.

* * * *

The white counselor lady is peeling a grapefruit today. It looks too big in her bony white hands. She gives me a pink section and I take it even though I hate grapefruit.

We don't say anything. I look around her walls. She's got a crazy postcard of five naked ladies all sectioned off in cubes and triangles, their elbows sticking out. They look like a geometry problem. One has a baboon face and another has on a scary mask—all of them women look like what they are or what they might become.

I've got my period and I feel worse off and uglier because of it. In case anybody ever wants to know, people don't listen to girls who aren't pretty. Mostly, that's just as well.

I wish there was a menstrual hut somewhere near the playground at my school. I read about those in a book about Africa. Women go in there and chat and drink hot tea and they get to stay away from everybody and everything. At my school, it seems like as soon as you get your first period, you get an abortion. I used to think it happened, naturally, just like that. I wish I could give my period to my mother so she wouldn't be pregnant anymore. I stare down at my shoes and sit there feeling covered in bright red blood. I'm glad that at least Sashay didn't get her period before she died.

The counselor is looking across her desk at me. "Cashay. Everything's gonna be all right. Really." She says it like she is trying to make it so, not for me but for herself.

"I hear that on TV all the time. 'Everything's gonna be all right.' Nobody ever says that to me."

She's picking the white membrane off her grapefruit. "Don't give up on everybody and everything just yet, Cashay," she says. "Not yet."

I look at her and I'm all, *Right, lady,* and I go, "OK. You just let me know when."

CHAPTER
5

"I've got one more string!" Sister Pigtails shouts.
She's holding up the end of a yellow string that leads
into a web of strings in the middle of the room at the
Catholic center. All the kids and mentors are standing
in a big circle holding the ends of strings. I'm here
because I promised my counselor I would give Sister
Pigtails one more try.

"Ah. Cashay! Here!" Sister Pigtails stands me next
to Juanita, who's got on a red tube top today. I hold
my bit of string while Juanita tells me this here's called
the spider web string game and when Sister says go

you start winding up your string until you get to the other end of it and that's how you get hooked up with your new mentor. I look over to the other side of the room. Sister Pam is over there and I'm praying—*praying*—I don't get with that woman again.

"We'll have no violence," Sister Pigtails says, and I swear she looks at me. "No pushing, no elbows. This isn't the NBA. When you find your partner, shake hands and introduce yourselves. The first pair to find each other will win a prize."

"What's the prize?" Juanita wants to know.

"You'll be excused from clean-up duty," Sister Pigtails says.

The grownups laugh while I look around, roll my eyes, and mutter to Juanita, "This is dumb."

I'm in an extra-special bad mood because even though I know Sashay is dead and all, I can't help but wonder and worry: Who is taking care of Sashay when I'm not? At night I talk and talk to her, and in the morning I wake up hugging my pillow, thinking it's Sashay.

"Ready? Set? Go!" Sister Pigtails says, all worked up over her stupid string game.

Juanita and I start rolling our strings. We're in no hurry. Sister Pam is already ducking under strings, getting tangled up with some little boy who falls over laughing. This little boy looks like a frog made into a boy and he whispers to himself all the time. Sister Pam starts to laugh too, but she's all fretting about making her ball of string as neat as it can be. I bet she wants to end up with that little boy because he's cute and happy and I'm pudgy and brown-beige and mad all the time and I can just feel her hating me and I start to hate hate hate her back.

In the middle of the room the little boy who fell over stands up and high-fives a white guy. "We won!" they both shout together.

Seems like everybody finds a partner all at once. Then I see Sister Pam coming toward me. She sees me too and she rolls her ball up slower and slower as she walks closer and closer. And then she ends her string with Juanita and I about bust a gut laughing. I'm so busy looking over Sister Pam looking over Juanita, who looks like one of those kiddie pop-up books about to open out of her tube top, I hardly notice the skinny white woman standing in front of me, grinning.

"Hi. My name's Allison!" She's all bubbly and pointy and it's too much. I have to step back. Her black hair is pulled back tight into a wet knot and she's got too much red stuff on her cheeks and she's wobbling on a pair of high heels and her short suit skirt is riding up and she can't stop smiling. I recognize her. She was one of the painters at the center when Sister Pigtails was showing us around. She was that sister trying so hard to impress one of the other man-painters. But this sister ain't no nun.

"Why your hair wet?"

"I just came back from swimming." She's got her eye on that white man with the little boy. "What's your name?" She doesn't care about my name, but I tell her anyway.

She looks at me. She's so jumpety, I'm wondering if she's on Ritalin. "Did you know your name means 'treasure' in French?" she says. "It also sounds a lot like *cash.*"

"I'm no treasure," I say. And her smile drops. Just like that, and she's one skinny frown. I want to bring the corners of her lips back up again, but I said what I said and I got to stick by it, so I go, "Names don't signify nothin'."

She smiles bright, brighter than the first time. Is she for real? Didn't she hear me?

She waves at the white man, takes my hand, and drags me on over. "Michael. Hey. Isn't this great?"

I'm thinking, *What's so great?*

Michael takes a look at me. He was one of the man-painters I'd seen, the one this Allison was trying to impress. He's all smiles too. What are these people on, anyway? Has Mr. Giggles been paying them a visit too? This Michael's little boy has already run off to play with the other little kids. "Who's this?"

"This is Cashay."

Michael checks her out. He's on to her, I can tell. This girl is loony, and I'm just watching, wondering what fool thing she'll do next.

"So you two going to be partners?" he says.

This Allison looks at me. Then she holds up her string and my hand goes up automatically because I forget I'm still holding on. "I guess we're sort of tied to each other now."

* * * *

Sister Pigtails takes Allison into her office while I wait outside, trying to listen to them talking about me. I catch a couple of things. *She's had a tough year* and *I don't know, Sister, she seems like a great kid, spunky and all, but . . .* Then I can't hear anything else, but when they open the door and ask me to come in, I can tell Allison got herself an earful. She's looking at me like she's a little bit scared and a little bit curious too.

"So," she says, "I hear you're pretty good at looking out for yourself."

"You two will be working together from now on," Sister Pigtails says. "I want you to tell each other a secret."

"What for?" I say.

"A secret?" Allison says. "What kind of secret?"

"Something you haven't told anyone else."

"Right now?" Allison says. She looks more scared than I am.

"Whisper it," Sister Pigtails says.

We both look at each other and think. Allison leans down. She smells like perfume, work, and coffee. "I've got a nasty-ass run in my stocking," she whispers, and I'm thinking, *That's it? That's your big secret?* Still, it is pretty funny, the way she says it in front of a nun and all.

"Cashay?" Sister Pigtails says. "Your turn."

I look up at the ceiling and think one last time. Then I look at Allison's ear. The inside's shiny and pink and there's one little pearl sitting on her earlobe. I whisper, "I failed seventh grade but I'm no dummy."

Allison straightens and nods like she's going to have to think on this.

"Now, Cashay, you brought your books with you?" Sister Pigtails says.

I pick up my book bag, like, *What's this look like to you?*

"All right, you two can use one of the free desks in the mentoring room. Go to it."

* * * *

We make ourselves comfortable. I pull out the book we use in Ms. Feeley's advanced algebra and it clunks on the table in front of us.

"Wow," she says. "That's a brick of a book."

We both stare at the book.

At the next table Sister Pam is lecturing Juanita, telling her how we're all stewards of the earth.

"You hear that?" Juanita says to no one in particular. "She wants me to be Martha Stewart!"

"Well then," Allison says. "Let's get started."

I don't like to talk while I work and it turns out this Allison can turn off the chat button when she gets down to work too. Except once her cell phone rings and she answers it.

She doesn't say much but I can hear a man on the other end, yelling *loud* about how if he hadn't listened to her five years ago, maybe now he'd still have some money or something to show for his money, like a BMW or a swimming pool. But no, now his stocks are down or sold and his money belongs to someone else or no one.

"Henry. Listen." She's calm, staring down at the floor. "It's Saturday and I'm not going to discuss your business right now." And she hangs up. Just like that.

"You know those things give you brain cancer," I say, looking at the cell phone.

"That's a myth," she says, turning the ringer off.

When I finish, Allison puts on a pair of glasses that make her look even better than she already does. Smarter. She looks over the pages of all the problems I've solved.

"So you're repeating seventh grade?"

"I flunked," I say. "Where does the money go when your stocks tank?"

She puts down my work and takes off her glasses. "Let's not talk about my work right now. Let's talk about you and your work. You know this stuff?"

"It's not too hard."

"And your test scores are really high."

"They are?"

"Yes. They are. They're high enough to make me think you could get into Benson's if you wanted to go there."

"That new school? In the Village? It costs money."

"It's going to be a magnet school, but it's public. It would prepare you for college. You would have to work hard. Study. But if that's what you wanted, maybe you could get in."

"How do you know so much about that Benson's?"

"My company's involved in the whole development."

"Even if I did get in, I can't go to college. I don't play basketball."

"Colleges have academic scholarships too."

"Someone else would pay for me to go to school? So I could just learn?"

"If you worked hard and you did well on the next round of tests and you applied. Maybe."

I look at this lady, this Allison with her legs and her nails and her smile and her cell phone. If I were white, all white, really white with blue eyes and hair the color they call corn silk, then maybe I could make something of myself. Maybe I'd be pretty, get a good job answering phones, wear skirts, and drink coffee from a white cup with a saucer after lunches in sit-down, tablecloth restaurants with the rest of my white girlfriends. We'd laugh and talk about our biggest problems—lipstick colors, boys, where to eat next—and we wouldn't ever worry about money, bullets, drugs, or our mamas.

"Are you doing time?" I ask.

She laughs. "For what?"

I shrug. "I don't know. Illegal stock tips?"

"Well, aren't you the knowledgeable one."

"I watch the news," I say. "I know the eighties are over."

She laughs. "So are the nineties. No, Cashay. I'm completely legit. I actually *want* to be here. With you."

I shake my head. "You *want* to be with that Michael dude."

She laughs, nervous. "What are you talking about?"

"How come you don't wear no jewelry?"

"I wear earrings," she says, touching the little pearls on her lobes.

"Nobody can see them."

"Jewelry gets in the way. I work in a man's world. You don't see many men wearing jewelry in my business."

"What exactly do you do?"

"I'm a stockbroker, and I don't have to make statements about who I am by what I wear."

I don't know what she's talking about. She just needs some bracelets or some necklaces or something, but I wonder: Where does she get all that confidence?

"What do you want to be when you grow up, Cashay? What do you want to do?"

When I grow up? I'm thinking, *What chance do I have of growing up at all? I'm lucky if I'm here on this earth five, maybe ten more years. Bonus years.*

"Would you like to go to college?"

"I want to go to college in Atlanta." It's the first time I've thought of college or of college in Atlanta. "My Aunt Jo'Neisha says we have relatives there and I saw the college once on TV. They have a marching band that plays *and* dances. I remember watching them with Sashay. I remember her saying how she wanted to go there."

"Cashay. Look. Sister Marie told me you flunked on purpose so you and your sister could go to Freemont together. I understand. It wasn't a bad plan. But things are different now."

I don't have anything to say to this.

I worry that Sashay is lonely at the cemetery with the rest of the dead. She doesn't know those people sleeping all around her. I want to go, climb in the white box, lie down next to her, hold her hand, and say, *Wait up now, Sashay. I'm here. I'll go to sleepy land with you. Don't close the gates yet, not without your big sister. Don't lock me out! I'm coming! I'm coming! Hold the door!*

"I'm sorry about your sister, Cashay. That must

have been awful." Her voice isn't all smiley this time. It has some gravel in it. "Let's do this. We'll get you ready to take that test for Benson's, so you have the option. At the very least you can show everyone you're no dummy."

CHAPTER
6

Saturdays I spend with Allison at the center. She wears jeans and pointy boots that make her teeter like someone on stilts. She wears such high shoes that she's never really walking on the ground. I guess she likes it up there. She wears light, close-fitting clothes and she always looks cold. She's skinny but she likes to have her body out. She comes with something called a venti coffee for herself and a grande chai tea for me. It's mostly milk and honey and I might could drink it forever.

"You got sixteen out of twenty," she says on this one Saturday.

"Dang. What'd I do wrong?"

"You just need to take your time, double-check your math."

I stare and stare at the page, but I can't see where I messed up. The numbers run into each other and don't look like numbers anymore. They look more like sentences I can't read, like they're in that Arabic language. Allison takes the page from me and folds it in half.

"You've put in a solid two hours, Cashay. What do you say we go blow off some steam?"

"You and me?"

"Yeah. Let's do something fun."

"Like go get some candy?"

"Maybe we can think of something better to eat."

"Good," I say. "My appetite's punching me and all I taste is my own spit."

Outside she walks a long-legged, ducky kind of walk. Cool until you look close. She always has on makeup and lipstick; she brushes her hair stick straight. Her smile makes me soft and when we walk I feel like a Twizzler stick, all loose and light and springy.

It's not warm, but it's not so cold anymore either. It's April, but that doesn't mean spring in Chicago. A jogger with headphones runs by. Then a man on a fast bike, and another on Rollerblades. Somebody's playing rap and they're singing nasty about themselves.

"You like Trina?"

"Is she a friend of yours?"

"She's a singer. That's her singing that song."

"Did you say singing or screaming?"

"She calls herself the baddest bitch," I say, laughing.

Allison listens for a minute, then says, "Civilized people don't talk like that."

I don't know why this doesn't make me mad.

After only a block, I see him. I see that gold-toothed T-Rex and he's all hooded and brooding and slouchy-like in his sweats and knit cap and gold chains and Fubu shoes. I hate him solid. I hate him hard and he catches sight of me. His nostrils flare, horse-like, and he looks like he's going to spit. I want him to come get me. I want him to so I can kill him myself.

"Do you know that man?"

"T-Rex? He ain't no man," I say. "He's a punk. He just goes around acting tough just so people don't think he's soft." He watches me watch him. "He killed my sister."

Allison looks at him, puts a hand on my shoulder, and says, "You know he did it?"

I think for a minute. "I didn't see him do it, but he was there. My counselor had me tell the police and they picked him up and held him for a few days. No one can prove anything, so now he's back on the street."

"That was a good, brave thing to do, Cashay. To go to the police." All the sudden, she's trying to hug me. "Wow," she laughs, almost falling off her stilt shoes. "It's hard to hug from up here."

Then she waves her arm and a cab appears from I don't know where. It just appears.

"Dang. You got you some long arms," I say, slamming the cab door shut, and I sit at the edge of the seat and watch T-Rex get smaller and smaller. If I were brave enough, I'd hunt him down and kill him my own self. But I don't want to even be next to that dark boy with his head all full of nasty hallways.

"You ever get tired of people?" I ask.

"Oh, yeah," Allison says. "But then, just when I'm ready to throw the towel in, I meet someone. Someone like you."

I look out the cab window and chase the buildings with my eyes as we speed uptown.

Fourteen years in Chicago and I never been in a cab. Here we are in the back all jostly and bouncy, and I can't help but laugh out loud with this driver's crazy driving and his island music playing. It's not a drive—it's a ride.

Then she goes, "Could you eat a cheeseburger?"
And I say, "I could."

* * * *

The burger in front of me has limp sweet onions hanging off it. I put ketchup, mayonnaise, and mustard on
that burger. I put a pickle on there too. I squish it all
down and I cut it in half and I take me a bite and have
me a moment of silence for that good, good burger.
I'm halfway through with my cheeseburger before
Allison even gets started. I'm not *trying* to eat fast. I'm
just trying to get to the taste faster. I wish I felt this
way all day, all the time, hungry and satisfied at the
same time.

"Is it good?" she asks.

"It's OK."

She laughs and the corners of her eyes turn tissue-
paper crinkly. "You eat the way I wish I could eat,"
she says, pouring something oily over her salad.

Outside, standing next to a dirty pile of snow, a
black guy keeps warm playing all kinds of music with
spoons, cookie sheets, pie pans for cymbals, and a bass
drum made out of a vegetable bin from a refrigerator.

"What do you do?" I ask Allison.

"I told you. I'm a stockbroker." She laughs, then shakes her head the way Aunt Jo'Neisha sometimes does. "This market. I *mean.* I got these clients calling, yelling at me, saying they're not going to be able to retire at forty. I'm like, Ooooh, I feel soooo bad for you." I could be her forty-year-old white girlfriend, the way she's talking.

She talks about people she does not like to work with and I eat and listen and tell her what's wrong with them and she says I'm incredibly wise for my age and I say, yeah, I guess so.

I color on the paper covering the table. You're supposed to at this place. I draw a cab with me and Allison in it.

"We're in a bear market," she says.

"I like bears."

"Bears meander. They're big and clumsy. I prefer bulls. Bulls charge forward."

"So that's what they mean with a bull market?"

Allison nods and goes on. She says this bear market just keeps going down. But still, she says it's not a slump or a depression. She calls it a correction. She pulls out a newspaper from her bag and shows me how to read the stock pages, how to look for your stock symbols or a bond quote. Together we pick stocks that she calls Cashay's Stock Picks, like it's something important. She shows me a company's quarterly report, also from her bag. She tells me about "the magic of compounding" and doubling your money and she says that sometimes the general interest of a company can exceed its value.

"And always *always* look for the positive bottom line. For everything," she says, winking.

I guess I'd wink back if I knew how.

Allison would have liked Sashay better than me. I can't remember Sashay ever being sad. I wonder what happened to me. Why is it that when I feel something, anything, I feel it so hard? Maybe that's why the neighborhood kids call me Brillo Pad. Maybe it never had nothing to do with my hair.

Allison doesn't talk about growth the way most women do. She's not talking weight or height or new dimensions. She's thinking about graphs and charts, numbers and money. She's got lemon breath and shoulders like a man's. This woman, Allison, she *thinks* like a man and I want to know how I can start thinking like that too.

She gives me the paper to look at and keep. She gives me the quarterly report to look at and keep too.

In the projects where I live, nobody talks about what's in the paper or the Middle East or the stock market or the economy. The news outside our walls is of no concern. It's more like, Who's got a light? Who's got a score? Where's the food? How many kids and what kind of dope?

"We can discuss your stock picks and this company next time we get together," she says.

She wants me to answer all kinds of questions. Who's running the company? How long has the company been in business? How profitable is it? How bad are the debts? What's the competition? And all the while I'm thinking, This isn't homework, this is real work, and I can't wait to get back to my room and read it.

"In the end, the market will correct itself," she says.

"How long can it last?" I have to ask. It's crazy to me. What makes a business cycle peak and then decline? What makes wind? Why are stop signs, blood, and sirens all red while go signs, grass, and money are green?

She shrugs. "It's been a while, but we're still paying the price after Nine-Eleven."

"I'm sick of hearing about Nine-Eleven."

"People died."

"You know any of them?"

She shook her head. "A lot of friends of friends."

"So? Why would *you* be sad?"

"Because they died. They were people."

"But you didn't *know* any of them."

"It's called sympathy. Maybe even empathy. I'm sad for others. You can be sad for other people. It was terrible and tragic. It's just really sad."

"Yeah, well, it doesn't help. Being sad doesn't help anything or anybody."

"Maybe not. Maybe yes. You never know. It just is. It's human." She looks all over my face and it makes me feel like I'm OK to look at. "I'm sorry that your sister died, Cashay. I'm very sorry for that. Does that make you feel better or worse?"

I don't say which. "It makes me feel nothing."

She just nods and waits. I know she's thinking about holding my hand, but she doesn't.

"You're not my sister," I say.

"I know that," she says. "I know."

* * * *

When our cab pulls up to a big building with steps and statues I ask Allison if this is college. She says, no, it's the Museum of Science and Industry.

"And for once, just for once, let's *not* go down into the coal mine?" she says.

I nod, thinking, *Why would I want to go down into a coal mine anyway?*

Outside, a circle of white kids my age are holding hands and praying. Someone outside the circle shouts, "Darwin lives!"

Stupid white girls with pink striped hair huddle together and take each other's pictures. I can't remember the last time anyone has taken a picture of me.

Allison stops at the museum shop and comes out with one of those disposable cameras. She reads from a sign out front: "'Do you dare walk through the pulsating heart of a twenty-eight-story-tall human?' I sure the hell will."

We step in through the right ventricle.

"I can put my arm through these holes," I say, reading the signs, sticking my arm in a plastic vein. Above, the atrium is squeezing, sending blood down through the wide-open tricuspid valve with its skinny white flaps. When the ventricle is full, it squeezes the tricuspid valve, then snaps shut, and blood flows through the pulmonic valve.

It's crowded inside this heart. It smells of sweat, plastic, people's shoes, and morning breath. The artery lights blink on and off. A lady tells her daughter that some people get married here. Somebody's used Big Gulp cup is right there on the left ventricle.

"This was way cooler when we were kids," Allison says.

I am in no hurry to get out even though it takes about three steps to walk through.

"That's because you got spoiled," I say. It's crowded and cramped in here and finally we both have to keep moving.

Allison asks a mother to take our picture in front of the heart. The woman looks through the little camera, then looks up at us.

"Can you move a little closer together?" the woman says.

Allison puts her arm around my shoulder. The side of my arm can feel her rib cage. She's sharp and bony but her skin is warm. I forgot how warm a body can be.

The lady takes our picture and gives Allison the camera.

We head toward the hatchery, but I can't look at the chicks and everybody cooing all over them. I'm mad and I don't know why.

Allison comes over and we walk to a bench. She picks up my hands. They're balled up into fists.

"Count to ten," she says.

I count to ten.

"Now take three deep breaths. Come on. I'll do it with you."

Some people look. I don't care. We breathe together.

"Now make a fist," she says. I make a fist with my right hand. I hold it up close to her face. Several people stop and stare and I imagine what they see: a black girl with dreadlocks fixing to punch out a skinny white woman.

Allison wraps her whole hand over my fist. "That's the size of your heart. I just read that. I never knew that before, did you? The size of your fist is the size of your heart."

I have to smile. My fists will look different to me from here on out. Now I will look at them and think of my heart.

We take the blue stairs down, and there we see an exhibit showing slices of a body. All around us are sliced sections of a man—his chest, his abdomen, even his head. He was sliced up like bacon and the slices look like so many T-bone steaks.

"Who is this guy?" I ask.

"You mean who *was* this guy. I think he was a prisoner who donated his body to science."

"I wouldn't want to get sliced up, would you?" I say.

Allison takes a deep breath. "You'd be here forever. That's one way of looking at it."

"This is nasty," I say, but I can't stop looking. I hear a mother tell her son that it's OK. "He didn't get killed for this. He was already dead."

"It's hard to tell, but I think he was a white man," I say.

"What's that goody-goody thing that Sister Pam says? 'We're all the same color inside'?" Allison takes a step forward to get a closer look at a slice of brownish liver, then she shudders.

I'm still trying to figure out the color of the dead, sliced-up man's skin. "I'm not black and I'm not white. I'm brownish."

"You're gold." Allison says this like it's a fact, not like she's trying to be nice. It's a nanosecond and I can't help but think this nanosecond, what she says, what's happening, should be lasting longer because of the way it makes me feel. Why do these in-between times that take place in stairwells have to be over so fast, while the mean times last so long?

"I'm way too young to look at this," Allison says. "Let's go."

* * * *

On the way out, we stop in the museum gift shop. In the center of the shop, there's a moving column filled with little license plates with names on them. I swirl the column around. Donald. James. Michael. Nancy. Cynthia. White people names. No Sashay. No Cashay. Allison is at the counter, getting out her wallet to pay for some mints. Two girls who look like ads for sugarless gum come over to pick out the license plates with their names on them. I go and look at the candy. Maybe Allison will buy me some Gummi Worms and Junior Mints if I ask nicely.

In the cab on the way back, she gives me a paper bag real casual-like. Inside the bag is a red notebook. On top of the red are gold letters, gold letters that spell out *Cashay*. I run my fingers across the letters. She tells me she had it special-ordered. They can do that. They can print a name like mine in gold.

"It's a calendar and a journal and an address book too. See? I put my name, number, and address in there. I was thinking you could maybe make a hostility log out of it so you can keep all your business together in one place. We can mark the days that we meet so you won't forget."

"I don't forget."

"I know."

"What's a hostility log?"

"You record your angry feelings."

I look at the book. I want to touch it. It *has* to be

red because people say anger is red, but mine feels more purple. "This was Sister Marie's idea, wasn't it?"

She shrugs, and then shows me how to get it started. After a while, she goes, "You don't like it, do you?"

"No. It's . . . I never saw my name on anything before. I never had my name on nothin' before—not like this."

She hugs me sideways.

"Well. Now you do."

I stare down at my name.

"That's you," she says.

"Lotta white space."

"Space meant to fill."

* * * *

The cab drive back home is a lot slower than the one from before, the one leaving. Our driver stops and hits the meter way before he's supposed to, and he and I both know why.

"We're not there yet," Allison says.

"This is close enough," he says.

"Oh, come on, man, one more inch," I say.

"Can't you go any farther?" Allison says.

"It's too dangerous, ma'am."

Allison sighs and looks around. "You think you can make it?"

"Yeah," I say to her. "It's not far." And it's not.

I start to open the door.

"I'll call you, OK?" Allison says.

"What about the place where a person lives?" I say all of a sudden. "Your property. Is that an asset or a liability?"

"It can be either. It can be both."

I look around me. "How do you turn a liability into an asset?"

"There are ways."

Before I leave, she reminds me to ask my teacher for a letter of recommendation to send to Benson's. She goes over how to ask people for favors, how to say *please* and *thank you* like you mean it, and I think of how good she must be at her job, how there's a difference between lying and having manners. She hugs me and says, "Love you." Her words hang in the air in cold clouds.

I step away from the cab and watch it drive off with Allison waving from the back seat. I can still smell her powdery, perfumy smell in the left-behind air. I put my hand up, like *Bye*, but I forget to shake it around in a wave. I don't think I've ever waved before. I watch Allison get smaller and smaller. The sun's going away and it's getting colder. The air has a refrigerator smell. The people around me are all hunched over and bent against the cold. There is only the hamburger taste left in my mouth to remind me of the day. But then that's gone too and there isn't anything left of the day or of Allison. It's like she was a dream.

She can give me a book with my name on it, then say this, say "Love you" and "You're gold," just like that. And to me. She makes me feel feelings again.

I can hear some birds chirping like they're talking about spring.

Aunt Jo'Neisha is walking across the playground with a stack of boxes.

"I got in! I got *in*," she says. We both know she's talking about the Village. I'm happy for Aunt Jo'Neisha but sad for me. "Don't you worry, girl. We're going to fix it so you and your mama can get in too." I ask if she needs help. She shakes her head and tells me to get on home before it gets too dark.

I wrap my locks around my neck like a scarf and get to walking.

CHAPTER 7

HOSTILITY LOG ENTRY #1

WHEN: Monday, 2:00 a.m.

SCENE: Mama takes a hit off a bong, blows out, asks me what I think she should name her baby.

THOUGHT: Why didn't they use birth control? Better yet, why couldn't they just leave each other alone?

FEELING: I hate her. I hate Mr. Giggles. I hate what their messed-up lives are doing to mine. I might not get into the Village because of them. We might lose the roof over our heads.

ACTION: I eat the rest of their potato chips.

INVOLVEMENT: I'm too damned tired to be involved.

HOSTILITY LOG ENTRY #2

WHEN: Thursday at some time too early to remember.

SCENE: Mama and Mr. Giggles wake me up with their noise.

THOUGHT: Why don't doors work? Why is he over here? Why doesn't he stay away?

FEELING: I hate that man, sniffing his fingers with his big nose, bad rap leaking out of the headsets in his little waxy ears.

ACTION: I punch a hole through Mama's wall. I am sorry I do it. Right away I am sorry, not just because my hand hurts but because I am the only one who cares what this place looks like and now I've gone and put a hole in the wall that I have to look at every day.

INVOLVEMENT: Too involved.

* * * *

I can see buildings reflected in puddles of water on the street, melted snow. It's May and all the buildings, all that tallness, are down on the ground now with the rest of us. Serves them right. At our meeting time on Saturday Allison reads through my log. She tells me not to worry so much about the wall. She says I don't have the inner resources to express my frustrations adequately.

"Hate is pointless and unproductive," she says. "When does hate yield anything worth anything? Now, anger. Anger you can make productive. It can give you energy, like you had with that wall, but you just have to focus your anger in the right direction. Not at your wall, but maybe at your work. Now let's get started."

* * * *

Saturday morning Mama doesn't want me to leave when she sees me fixing to. She yells, "Cashay! Hey, Cashay! You come and help me with this." She's out there in the hallway of the building, hammering, boarding up the place Aunt Jo'Neisha left behind. I see faces poking out, looking me over like I'm the bad one here, like Mama's the one always around cooking and cleaning and I'm never helping out.

"I gotta go, Mama."

"You ain't goin' nowhere till we board this place up."

"Mama . . ." The outside smells like wet dog and puke.

"Don't you yell your voice at me, girl," Mama says. "Your Aunt Jo'Neisha up and leaves 'cause she too good for this place 'n' I ain't gonna let nobody think they can just move in without paying rent. Now come on and help me with these boards."

Used to be I couldn't tell Mama was high. I just thought she was happy. She came into my room by accident late one night and I could see her white teeth.

"Mama? Why are you smiling like that?"

"Like what, baby doll?" she said, crawling into bed with me. That was back when being high made Mama nice.

Now her eyes say she is looking for dope, and trying to guess what goes on in her drugged-out head is wearing me out.

The yellow cab comes and I see it stop at the end of the block.

"I gotta go."

I can hear my mama call after me. I can hear her say, "Where you think you goin', girl? Now you leavin' me too?" I can feel her eyes on my back.

"Cashay!" she calls, crazy mad.

"Yo. Cashay." I run right into T-Rex, who's smiling his gold-tooth smile, wearing a red and yellow bandanna tied around his head like he some girl. Gang colors or whatever. He holds my arms, like we're maybe planning to dance or stop and chat.

"I been looking for you, Cashay," he says, twisting my wrists in his rough hands. "I hear you been telling stories on me. Telling stories to people like the police. What that all about? Don't you know we're friends?"

"You're not my friend, T-Rex."

"OK then. Future employer. You can still work for me, Cashay. Because you know why? If you don't . . ." But I set myself loose and I keep on run run running toward that cab like it's my golden pumpkin, and T-Rex, he's yelling out after me, "You think you goin' uptown? Girl, you goin' nowhere but down and out, and I'm taking you there."

* * * *

Inside the cab, Allison checks the address she has written in her book.

"Got your pencils?" she says.

I tap my coat pocket. "Pencils." I got candy corn

too, but I don't tell her that. I'm wearing sweatpants with a drawstring, ready to be comfortable. I like my waistbands loose.

"Nervous?"

I shake my head.

"Not even a little?"

"A little. Maybe."

"Good," she says. "A few nerves are good. Pumps up the adrenaline."

We both take a deep breath, then look out the window. Even though it's officially spring, the parking lots are dotted with brown snow mountains from all the leftover plowed-up snow. Somebody's gone and topped all those dirty snow mountains with shopping carts. Allison gives me a sucker the color of a go light to get me going.

"Pythagorean theorem," Allison says, still looking out her window.

I see a little girl jumping rope, doing cradle rock. She's got plaits like Sashay, but it's not Sashay. I can feel water in my eyes, and my nose stings. "A squared plus B squared equals C squared."

I can feel Allison's hand patting me on the leg.

I like formulas. They calm me down. Math explains what you don't know. Not much else does that so good.

"What's the area of a parallelogram?"

"Base times height."

"The perimeter of a polygon?"

"The sum of the length of each side."

"You're going to do great," she says. "I just know it."

* * * *

The classroom at Benson's is yellow. There are maybe twenty other girls already there in their seats, ready to take the test. Allison stands with me at the door.

"I'll meet you here when you're finished. We'll go get something to eat."

I take a seat in the back row. Allison waits, gives me a corny thumbs up. I smile, and mouth *Bye*.

"She walks funny," some chocolate-colored smart-ass says, and I'm ready to get mad, but then I see that she's smiling. I recognize what this girl is thinking and feeling and I smile too, and we watch Allison walking away, fast and with her chin up, like she's shouting, *I defy you!* And everybody around her is looking like, *What the . . . ?* and I'm thinking, *There she goes. She's some funny, duck-walking, skinny-assed, homework-helping white stockbroker. And she's mine.*

* * * *

Over lunch, after the test, Allison gives me a desk set that's wrapped up together in one package—what she calls a blotter, a stapler, a hole punch, a letter opener, ruler, pen, number-two pencils in a holder, and even a Scotch tape dispenser. I keep it wrapped up because it looks so nice like that, all pieced together like a puzzle, neat and tight under the cellophane. I don't want to see it unfold and fall apart.

"You should know all about that burger," she says when our lunches come. "You read the research reports on the Burger Factory, remember?"

"Oh, yeah."

"We're taking them public."

"What's that mean?"

"Means we're handling the initial stock sale."

She goes on about the company and the stock. She's talking crazy to me again and I shake my head, trying to make it make sense.

"We're selling shares of the company and we hope those shares go up in price. If they go up, we all make money."

"What makes the shares go up?"

"When they sell hamburgers."

I watch Allison take a big bite out of her burger. I've never seen her eat anything but a salad. She eats that burger the way it deserves to be eaten. "They'll do good," she says, ketchup and mustard dripping from the corners of her mouth, and we both laugh.

"Sashay likes grilled cheese sandwiches," I say, not thinking. It has been so long since I've said her name out loud, and the word almost gets stuck in my throat. "Those little colored toothpicks that come stuck in them always make her smile."

"What else does Sashay like?"

I look at Allison. I want to thank her for talking about Sashay like this but I don't know how to thank. I tell her how Sashay likes mint mouthwash and cinnamon toothpaste at different times in the day. I tell her how she eats diced pineapples from the can on Sundays and how she likes to sit on the sofa and sniff her feet.

Allison folds and unfolds a dollar bill, staring down at it quiet-like.

"Sashay's dead, Cashay. You know that, right?"

I nod. "I know."

I watch Allison to see, but she just blinks and keeps on. "Dead doesn't have to mean dead and gone."

"I shouldn't've walked us so close to Buddha and T-Rex that day."

"That couldn't be helped, Cashay. They were on your route home."

"I should've moved her along faster."

"You can't blame yourself. It's just something that happened. A terrible thing happened. It wasn't your fault that Sashay was shot and killed."

She says those words just like that. Out loud. In front of me. And I don't hate her for saying them and I don't get mad. No. I am glad she says them. It's like I was waiting for someone to say them so that I could feel them. And now I do. And I sit there, still, letting what she said fall and settle all over me, and that's when I first know what that word *quiver* means.

"Why do you do that?" I say after a while. "Why do you stare at that dollar like that?"

She looks up from the dollar. "It helps me focus. See this?" She points to the cut-up pyramid with the floating eye. I never looked at that before. *"Annuit coeptis,"* she says. "That means 'Providence has favored our undertakings.'"

"Is that some kind of prayer?"

"It just helps me. That's all I know."

"I thought prayer had something to do with God, not money."

"People are capable of making their own luck," she says, putting the dollar away. "So? How do you think you did on the test?"

"It was hard." I think about it. "Maybe Providence favored *my* undertaking, though."

Allison smiles. "Benson's is going to be a good school because it's going to challenge students."

"What's the hardest thing you ever had to do?"

"I don't know. Every day is hard."

"I mean the *hardest*."

She thinks about this. "Getting my MBA, maybe. It was a lot of work."

"What's a MBA?"

"A master's degree in business. It's what you do after college if you want a good job in business."

I think on this. More school *after* more school.

"I think we need a game plan. Let's figure out what *you* want and how you're going to get it." She takes a pen from her purse and writes on a napkin. "OK. What do you want?"

Want? What do I want? I want to get past fourteen. Period.

"Just regular stuff everybody wants."

"Like what?"

"A cell phone, for one."

"A cell phone? What are you going to do with a cell phone?"

"Call people."

"Like who?"

"You."

Allison writes down "cell phone" on the napkin.

"What about you? What do you want?" I ask.

"Me? Right now, I guess . . ." She looks around. There's a couple at another table. The woman's leaning toward the man, saying, "It's not what we wanted, but it's what happened to us."

"I don't know. I really feel like I have everything." She gets all fidgety and I don't know why. "Maybe I want a husband. I don't know."

"You have a boyfriend?"

She looks around, laughs, starts to eat more burger, stops, and looks at her watch. "Every now and then. See, the only way I've ever gotten anything was through work and money. I don't know much about love or even friendships. It's like, I don't know. All I know is that they both take up a lot of time, and for me, time is money. OK. Enough about me. Where do you want to be in ten years?"

"Ten years?"

"Five. Five years."

"Why does every white person ask this?"

"One year. What about next year?"

"I don't know. Maybe right here, where I am now."

"At the Burger Factory?"

"Maybe I just want to still *be*." Then I think on this some and tell her that maybe I'd like to live in the

Village, but I can't right now because Mama's piss has drugs in it and she's lost her job and now she's fixing to have herself another baby and we need to have an annual income of at least $20,000 a year.

Allison crumples up the cell phone napkin. "Cashay, when did all this happen?"

"It's always happening."

* * * *

Inside the apartment, Mama is on the sofa.

"Hey, Mama. How you do?"

"I feels nice."

"You clean?"

"Yeah," she giggles. "I done took a bath."

"You know that's not what I mean, Mama. That stuff's gonna kill you. Ain't no old junkies."

"Leave me alone, girl. I tol' you. I feels nice right now and I'm gonna stay that way for as long as I can."

I use a mop to clean up the puke in the corners, even on the walls. I spray the air with Windex.

A stack of bills sits on the arm of the sofa next to Mama. I'm thinking, *Why do we have bills? Who's buying? And with what?* For the first time in my life, I take an interest in what's in the mail.

Credit card bills. Who's got a credit card? There are charges for a TV and groceries I haven't seen and for clothes I'm not wearing. It's all in Mama's name.

"Mama? When did you get a credit card?"

She waves me away. "I don't have no credit card, girl. Now take this and put it in the icebox." She gives me a pillow.

I go to Mama's purse and look in her wallet. No credit cards there. I can only think of one explanation: Mr. Giggles. I take the bill and call the number, say there's been a mistake, say my card's been stolen, say I want to cancel. The woman is nice. I tell the truth and she takes it all in. I hang up, hoping this doesn't mess up our chances even more to get into the Village.

Mama. She likes crunchy Cheetos and popcorn sprinkled with sugar. She likes her dirty pink slippers. That's about all I know now. I know more about Allison than I know about Mama. Mama's got a credit card bill of $10,000 and we don't have more than $20 between us. We are in some mess. Exactly where are we on this business cycle? What's the direction of interest rates? What are my economic indicators? For the first time I really get what *liability* means.

Mama used to walk so fast, we couldn't keep up. She used to tell me how it was when I was inside her, getting hiccups, kicking and rolling around, keeping her up. She laughed when she told me this, like it was no big deal, like it wasn't all that amazing.

"Ma? What do you want?"

"A Pepsi. Get me a Pepsi."

"No. I mean, what do you really want, like on down the line?"

Maybe she wants a new dinette set. Maybe she wants to fix up the place, paint the walls, and get new throw pillows.

"Oh, baby. I can't think like that."

"Why not?"

She looks at me. "You know why, Cashay." I listen to her more when she doesn't swear. She knows this.

The first time my stock picks went down I wanted to sell, but Allison says that's a common mistake. "Just because a company has a momentary lapse doesn't mean you should get rid of it altogether. Think of what it has to offer. Consider its future. You've got to think long term," she says. "Look at the company. If it's a solid company with plenty of resources, if its decline has everything to do with the bad economy and inflationary pressures, hold on for the long haul. Always think long term."

"How long can a recession last anyway?" I asked Allison.

"You never know what might happen," Allison told me.

I'm trying to remember a time when Mama wasn't thinking about drugs or men, back when Sashay was alive and she was thinking about us. But right now? Right this minute? Mama is in the dead middle of a bad economy herself, and I sigh, knowing I'm just going to have to wait out this particular business cycle.

"We're lucky," Mama says out of nowhere.

"Yeah? How's that?"

"Things could be worse. Look at us. We still have our legs and we can see."

I nod and let her keep on with the TV.

My mama. She thinks all a person needs to keep on keeping on are legs and eyeballs. She might know about keeping alive but she doesn't know about living well. And I'm not talking living with more stuff like cable, real soda pop, and a nice sofa. I'm talking about being happy.

Sometimes I wish I'd never been happy the way I was happy with Sashay because now I know what that feels like.

I sit down next to Mama and stare at the TV and my head is full up with all the things I need to say but can't. The show's about tornadoes, twisters going all over the place, messing up things. The man is talking about wind velocity, and then he says something about ground truths. That's what he says is important to people who study damage: ground truths.

Mama's hand lotion is on the table and I squirt some on my hands, and then I take Mama's hands and rub them in mine.

Sashay was darker than I am but our skins were the same kind of dry. It used to be that Mama would put lotions on us after our baths and we hated when she did this because the lotion was so cold. So she had this game. She made her hands heavy and slippery with lotion and we grabbed hold and she said, "Oh, hold on, else you'll fall into the hot lava!" and our hands always slipped out and we fell back on the bed, giggly and smooth.

"Hold on," I whisper now to Mama sitting on the sofa beside me. "Else you'll fall into the hot lava." But she doesn't hear me and I just keep on rubbing her hands in mine, pretending to watch the next show that's supposed to be funny.

CHAPTER
8

Mama's in the bathtub screaming, "It's time it's time!"

"Mama," I scream. "That baby's not supposed to come till July."

"I'll go boil water," Mr. Giggles says. I can see now they have no kind of plan.

"You get us a cab," I say. "We going to the hospital."

"Latisha if it's a girl. William if it's a boy," Mama's saying while I get her ready. She sucks on one of those hot-dog-smelling cigarettes. "Softens the pain," she says to me.

* * * *

At the hospital, we check in and they roll Mama into a delivery room. People I've never seen—a doctor and a nurse—poke her with needles and ask her all kinds of questions.

"Hey, y'all. This baby wants *out*," she's saying.

A nurse is putting scrubs on Mr. Giggles.

I hear the doctor and the nurse talking. I hear *She's got a history* and *crack*. I hear *preemie* and *blood sample*. I hear *amniotic fluid sample*.

They roll Mama's bed with her on it out and into another room. She calls out to me, talking nonsense. "Call me so I come get done." Then she says to the nurse, "It burns. Am I on fire?"

"Jesus," Mr. Giggles says, laughing, following the bed. "What they give her?"

I wait outside the room they take her in. I can hear Mama wail while that baby splits and shrieks its way into the world. I can't help but think about something so cute and little-baby-like coming into the world in such a loud and bloody way. Do all new starts have to happen out of violence?

"Cashay?"

I turn around to see who this voice belongs to. A white woman with a notepad is there. I recognize this woman but I don't know why or how.

"How are you doing? How's your mother? You remember me? Linda Johnson from Social Services. I was your caseworker a while back. The doctor paged me."

"Paged you? What for?"

"Well, you know. Your mother has a history. And they're concerned about the baby. It's against the law to be on drugs while you're pregnant, Cashay. Your mother came into this hospital high and there's a pretty good chance that the baby will be born addicted."

"Babies can't be addicted. They just babies."

I hear crying and crying and crying. Baby crying. I look at this Linda Johnson. I say, "It's supposed to be crying. It's a baby." But I know I don't sound so sure and the crying keeps on and on and on.

A nurse comes out of that room and gives Linda Johnson a look. "You have a baby brother," she says to me. Then she says to Linda Johnson, "We're going to have to start him on paregoric every four hours."

"What's that? What they gon' do?" I'm trying hard to take this in. I want to make everybody slow down so I can take it all in.

The nurse bends down close to me and she doesn't smell too mediciney. "You see, Cashay, when addicted babies are born, they're so hypersensitive that noise and light and even touch are amplified by thousands and it's all just a big bang to them. They usually just cry and cry like your brother's doing now. What we're going to do is keep him swaddled in a nice, soft blanket and put him in a quiet place with very little light. Since he's going through withdrawal, we'll put a little medicine in his bottle when we feed him. Paregoric is like a morphine opiate that will calm him down."

"You gonna drug him?"

The nurse looks to Linda Johnson then to me. Now she sounds mad. "Your brother is going through withdrawal from the drugs your mother took while she was pregnant. We have to treat him as though he is an addict."

"Can I hold him?"

The nurse shakes her head. "I don't think that's such a good idea. He's in a pretty bad way and we need to check for any neurological damage." She stands and starts whispering to Linda Johnson, then leaves.

"What? What? What she say?"

"Your mother's going to have to enter a treatment center. She needs help, Cashay. She hasn't been a very

responsible mother—to you or to your brother. She's
got to stop using drugs. While she's there, the state
has to put the baby in foster care."

I'm thinking. I'm looking, but I don't see nothing.

"You'll need a foster home too, Cashay."

The doors open up while doctors go in and out. I
peek in to see a little brown squalling thing in a bun-
dle of white. He was born just so he could cry.

Mr. Giggles is rocking back and forth inside his
green scrubs, his hands over his ears. Mama's asleep
in her rolling bed. The nurse is looking at Mama, filling out a report, talking to a doctor. The way they're
acting, I know something else besides the baby is on
their minds.

* * * *

Since everybody's talking drugs it shouldn't surprise
me to see the police, but it does. Policemen don't look
right in a hospital, but here come two walking down
the hall and into Mama's room. They arrest Mama,
and when they see a pipe and a bag of dope in his
pocket, they arrest Mr. Giggles too, and while they're
doing that and he starts complaining, I slip away.

Now I wish I'd taken care of Mama and killed Mr.

Giggles so she couldn't get the dope she took to addict this here baby brother of mine. I don't even know what I should be wishing I did. It's just terrible terrible terrible and I'm sad sad sad and it's like I'm having my own personal 9/11.

That night I ride home on the El, looking at all the people squished together. A woman holding a baby, a man reading a book, a lady asleep, an old man with a box of cigars, a workman in his jump suit leaning against an old lady trying to knit. I squint and they all look like one line, like a graph with numbers, like those stock market reports you see in the paper. I don't see shapes or different kinds of clothes, just one solid line. The way I see it is everybody looks different but everybody is like a part of our own selves and we're all this one big whole body moving around here on the earth.

I don't want to go to Allison or to Aunt Jo'Neisha with my troubles. They'll think I want to move in, and even if I do, that would be no good. The way they have their lives set up, why would they want me coming in and messing it all up?

When I finally do get home, I fall into my bed, and just before I fall asleep I consider thumbing a ride on the Dan Ryan Expressway and wonder how far south I could get.

* * * *

I spend the day at school, sleeping in Ms. Feeley's class. She lets me. Sometimes, it's like she knows everything.

I wake up in time to see Linda Johnson outside talking to our principal. I ask Ms. Feeley for a hall pass to the girls' room, then I slip out of school and set myself to walking.

CHAPTER 9

Later that night, when I get home, the place looks terrible bad. Before we went to the hospital, Mama and Mr. Giggles left empty bottles and cans everywhere. The room smells like an ashtray and I up the windows to let in some air.

I can't eat another can of chicken noodle soup. I can't look at another pink Sno Ball. Sometimes a girl just gets tired of these foods. I need something good for me. I pour a bag of beans from Aunt Jo'Neisha into a pot, and before I put the water in, I run my fingers through the beans the way Sashay liked to do. This feels so good it gives me the shudders.

I turn the radio on, fooling with the station channels and settling on some station where a lady is talking Roth IRAs and the potential for appreciation. I listen to the radio program while I follow the directions on the bag of beans and start a good-smelling soup.

I can't find my hostility log, so I get out a sheet of blank paper and I write.

HOSTILITY LOG ENTRY #23

WHEN: Late, I forget what day.

SCENE: After the hospital, after they take away Mr. Giggles and roll Mama into a special room where she can't have any visitors, after my baby brother cries and cries and cries.

FEELING: Older than I am. Big, hairy, mean, and hard. Too hard.

ACTION: Can't, but wish I could talk to Sashay, put my head in her lap, let her flip my locks through her fingers and rub them with aloe vera juice and hair gel, get her to twist those locks tighter to make them hold.

* * * *

All week I am able to hide out on the streets in the afternoon and dodge Linda Johnson and still go back to school most mornings. One afternoon the principal calls me to the office. Ms. Feeley gives me a look like she's saying, *OK, time's up. I can't cover for you anymore.* I leave her room with my head down, but I head for the girls' room instead, then slip out the back door exit and I walk. I don't go home because I know Linda Johnson will end up there looking for me. I walk the triangle, heading up Division, turning on Larrabee, then Evergreen, and coming back on Burling. Then I start all over again, all the while thinking about how we live only a few blocks from the Gold Coast and right around the corner from streets named Fairplace and Bliss. When it's dark, I sneak back home and sleep there.

Buzz saws and jackhammers and bulldozers scream every morning and all week the market goes down down down. And every other day I wait at the Catholic center for Allison, where she sits down and we get to work. I don't talk about any of my problems because I want to forget that I have them, and when I'm with Allison, I do. But one day Allison doesn't come.

"Her office left a message," Sister Pigtails tells me. "She's in a meeting and has to cancel." Sister Pigtails offers to help me herself, but I stay and do the work alone. I'd rather work alone than with Sister Pigtails.

I go home and consider my organizing principles. I make my bed now. I tell myself there is no more time for fast food, so I quit eating it. Friday I walk to the Village office just to read the bulletin boards and talk up the lady behind the desk. I know that word must have got out about Mama, but no one says anything to me. I know I can keep the apartment until they tear it down, as long as I don't make money or I don't report my earnings. Those are the rules. If I don't follow the rules, they can kick me out with less than a month's notice.

One week later, I see Linda Johnson again outside my school, talking to my old counselor, the principal, and Ms. Feeley this time. I get out before they see me and I run home and lock myself in. Later, that Linda Johnson shows up outside the door of our apartment, knocking, calling my name, asking me to let her in. She's saying she's found a nice place for me. She's saying I'll be OK. I'm already OK. I'm not ready to listen to what she has to say about foster homes. I don't answer the door.

I can't go to school. I can't visit my school counselor and I can't stay inside the apartment because that Linda Johnson will be there for sure now, every day, looking for me, or else Ms. Feeley and the principal will turn me over. Early the next morning I go outside on the playground and sit on the bench, looking through an old paper for coupons. A couple of boys shoot hoops. The woman sits playing checkers with herself next to the men playing dominoes. A homeless man walks by and he looks at me like I'm sitting on his bed or something.

"Yo. Cashay." T-Rex is swaggering toward me, angry-like. It looks to be he could knock me down with one finger. He dropped out of school way back when he was in elementary school. No one even knew where he lived. I think of him only as T-Rex, with no home, no mama, and no daddy. I can't even picture him as a kid, even though he's maybe seventeen.

I might as well be all alone. I am exactly in the wrong place.

I get up. My fists are closed so tight, they're rocks. They are my only weapons. I could go after him now. I take a deep breath. In my head, I hear Allison counting to ten for me, and I wish she'd quit it. Sashay used to sing when she was scared and I start in. *"Kookaburra sits in the old gum tree,"* I sing. *"Merry merry king of the bush is he. Laugh, Kookaburra, laugh, Kookaburra. How gay your life must be. Ha ha ho ho hee hee."*

I want to run. I think to myself, *I'm not scared of T-Rex,* but I know I am.

Then I hear the woman playing checkers start to sing. The men playing dominoes join her. They are all looking up, singing "Kookaburra," nodding toward me, as though they are saying, *Go on, go on.* I sing with them, and now we are all there on the playground singing about a laughing bird while I walk straight ahead and right past T-Rex. He steps back—he steps back!—because he thinks *we're* the crazy ones.

Maybe I'm not such a coward for not going after Sashay's killer after all. Yield *has different meanings, depending on the investment,* Allison once told me. *You've got to think about the markets. You've got to think about the rate of interest and futures. You've got to say to yourself, What am I going to get out of this?*

I step into a phone booth while T-Rex watches. I can still hear the others singing. I punch in Allison's number. The phone connection is fuzzy and some lady that doesn't sound real is asking me for twenty-five cents that I don't have. The sky is clouding over and I'm feeling cold and chappy.

All around me the Village and the new buildings and stores on the other side of the projects are lit up and open, and there, on the corner, right between

Dominick's and Starbucks is a brand-spanking-new Burger Factory. I see the Help Wanted sign hanging in the window. I watch one, two, three, four people go in and place an order. If I walk in there and ask for a job, will they laugh at me?

I try to look calm, strolling out of the phone booth. T-Rex starts to cross the street to where I'm at, like he's got some business to take care of with me. Then he quits walking after me and shouts, "Cashay, now or later, I'm gonna get you back for ratting on me. You never should have done that, sister. You don't go telling no cop about T-Rex. That only gets you in the grave."

I head straight for the Burger Factory like it's Oz or something, and I go in and tell them exactly what I need.

CHAPTER
10

I start work at the Burger Factory. May's over and there aren't but a few weeks of school left, but I don't go back there because I don't want to meet up with that Linda Johnson. I'm hoping Ms. Feeley will understand. I don't go to the Catholic center either.

At the beginning, it's my job to clear off tables, wipe down surfaces, chairs, and the floors, fill the saltshakers and ketchup bottles. Then later, I'll get to take orders behind the counter. To my mind, it's what I've been doing since I was born, except for now I'm getting paid.

The others, they smoke dope in the freezer so no

one will smell it, but I stay away from all that nonsense because this job has already saved my life once.

I polish the napkin holders and see my reflection. I get a fix on my looks. With my dreadlocks pulled back into a pigtail and stuffed inside a net, which is all stuffed inside a hat, I look a lot like someone else. Will I turn into this person I am disguised as? Or will I end up living in a box in the summer, sleeping on the El in the winter, standing out on Dearborn with my hand out, hoping maybe somebody has something to give me?

I put one napkin holder on each table. I give every table a ketchup and a mustard too. Allison says I have a strong sense of order. I step back and look at the shiny tables and floors. I watch people eat. Sometimes I look out the window and see T-Rex staring back.

* * * *

It surprises me when I get to my building late and I see Allison, not the social worker, standing outside waiting for me.

"You left this at our last session," she says, holding up my red hostility log. I look all over her face. I can't tell if she read it or not. Probably she did. Probably she got worried and that's why she's here.

"Where did you get that Burger Factory hat?" Allison says.

"They gave it to me. I got a job. I'm working there."

"Cashay, you're kidding. You're fourteen. How'd you get a job?"

"I lied on the application, 'n' they were so busy, nobody checked."

She's looking like she isn't sure if this is good news or bad news.

"I've talked with the sisters at the Catholic center. I've talked with your teacher Ms. Feeley too. Then somebody called me. A social worker named Linda Johnson."

"You been busy."

"Cashay, why didn't you tell me? About your mom and all."

"Nothing to say." I reach in for mail. Nothing. We head up the stairs.

"I could have helped, you know. You should at least give your friends the chance to help out."

"We live on the fourth floor," I'm saying while she follows. "I always take the stairs 'cause you never know who you gonna get stuck with in an elevator."

"'We'? Cashay. Your mother's at a prison rehab center."

I knew this and I did not know this. How can that be?

* * * *

In the cab to Allison's I tell her that I'll sleep over just for this one night, that I can take care of myself just fine with my job and school, and she nods, agreeing, saying how she'll see. Then I ask her how the Burger Factory's doing.

"The stock? Holding steady. It's about the only stock that's not getting slammed."

"I bet people still want to go out, but they don't want to spend so much money anymore," I say.

"I bet you're right," Allison says.

I haven't talked to a person in a long while. I have so many questions about business cycles and the economy that Allison has to tell me to slow down.

"But I don't get why there has to be these recessions and depressions," I say.

"We don't live in a perfect economic world," she says. "If we did, everything would always be going up and up. Sometimes the market has to go down just so it can go back up again. It's a roller coaster."

* * * *

She lives in one of the olden buildings that look out onto the lake near a part of town called the Magnificent Mile. The new buildings are tall and glassy and steely. Hers is brown and brick with iron fencing, a patch of green grass, and a nice doorman who's quick with an umbrella. I see one black man with a briefcase come into her building. His hair is cut short, close to his head. In the elevator going up, he looks at me and I look at him.

Her place is light and clean and colorful. The ceilings and windows are all up high so you can look and think.

She's got a bowl of lemons in her bathroom for no reason other than to have the color yellow around. While I'm looking, she's talking about some guy she used to date who called her late and wanted to talk about why they broke up.

She's shaking her head, saying, "These guys. They go to therapy and *then* they want to talk."

"Were you with that guy? From the center? The one you painted with?" I want Allison to keep on talking about herself. I don't want her to ask about me.

"Michael? I wish. No. This one was Ted. We're at

this dinner, right? All the guests are seated. During the salad, he tells me he has a cash flow problem. Then he starts sucking on my earlobe."

"Ewww," I say.

"I know. It's like, I don't want to hear about your finances."

"I said 'eww' because he's got his mouth on your ear."

"I know, and at the table. People are there, *eating!*"

I laugh. Her problems are funny because nobody dies.

On her kitchen wall there's a big picture of a black boy holding a dead fish. Next to a mirror in her bathroom there's a picture of women wearing saggy, old-fashioned-looking bathing suits. "It's a nice picture for a black-and-white," I say, because she's looking at me like she needs me to make some kind of commentary.

"I'll take you to school tomorrow, first thing. Let's get some sleep."

She gives me a pair of flannel pajamas to change into. They're big on her, but they'll fit me fine.

I have myself a look-see around. She doesn't cook. She eats fruit and she drinks Diet Coke and if she gets really hungry she goes out to dinner. She has a lot of desks and chests with empty drawers.

"So what do you think?"

I open a door. It's a closet that's really a room, a room full of shoes. She turned this room into a closet when most people would turn this closet into a room.

"It's kind of weird."

"Weirdness is part of the human condition."

"You've got a lot of"—I look around—"shoes. But no food. You must have a gazillion dollars."

"You can meet your goals if you learn to invest wisely." She sighs and drinks water. "I don't know who said that."

"I don't know," I say. "I wonder how it will all be. For me. For my mama and everything."

"It's late. We're both tired. Let's think about this tomorrow when our heads are clear." She looks skinnier than usual, and bone tired. She looks like paper with cursive writing on it going all scratchy.

"Who raised you?"

"My father raised my sister and me alone. It wasn't easy for him either. He was an air-traffic controller. Did I ever tell you that?"

I shake my head no.

"He was a good guy. Told me always to keep your lights on, stay focused, and your planes won't wreck."

"He dead?" I don't know how else to ask.

Allison nods. "A few years ago."

"You miss him?"

"Sometimes I forget to think about him enough."

I know what she means. Sometimes I'm glad not to think about Sashay, then I do and I feel bad that I didn't think about her.

"Any idea when you're going to hear from Benson's?"

"They gonna send me a letter."

We walk through her apartment. Her living room walls are a special color she calls azure something. I don't know—it seems right to take her hand, and I do. She's got art all over her rooms. There are more pictures and paintings of crazy things like shirt collars and writing.

"Hieroglyphics," she says.

"Hyacliffs?" I say.

"Hieroglyphics. It's an old language, a mix of different languages, I suppose. I don't think anyone's ever figured out how to translate it. It's written—you can't speak it."

The window next to the painting is fogged up, and with her finger she writes "Cashay." It makes me smile.

"You know what it means, right?"

"You already told me. Treasure."

"It's also a stamp. A mark of genius."

I think about this. I look around her rooms. Pretty rooms with good, clean sheets and nice-smelling soaps and a clean kitchen with no pots or pans. Her place is like a special place to hide. Anything ripped or broken is probably thrown out or given away or moved to the back of a closet. That's a good life right there.

In this apartment? With this white woman? I get full of sadness and I don't know why.

She has cable, but she says she only watches the news. Each window has a different view of the city. From her living room, you can see the lake. From her bedroom and dining room, you can see the city. I've never seen Chicago like this, all lit up. The only places you can see are the ones bright enough to be seen, and the rest, the rest is just in the dark, like it doesn't even exist. I imagine this is the way the world works. And this, well, this just stuns me for a minute.

Allison walks into those museums, the stores, the restaurants down there, and she is not scared of the people, the weird-colored walls, the white tablecloths, the expensive food. She is comfortable, sometimes even bored. I look down at the lit-up part of the city. Down there? That's her world, and I wonder how and when it became her world. It is more her world than it is mine. She is white. I am not. She is rich. I am not. She is single. I have Mama and all that comes with Mama.

I don't want to be one more person down there, walking the streets, looking for stuff. I want more than just stuff. I don't know what I want to do or be, but I want to show somebody who I am and what I am made of.

"You know, Cashay, you could live here," Allison says. "With me. I've already discussed this with Linda. I said I'd look after you. I gave her my word."

I know my answer to that straight off. "No. It doesn't feel right."

"Maybe not long term, but it has to do for now. Until Linda can sort through the paperwork. We'll see."

I don't want to hurt her feelings, but her place might as well be Mars. "If I had a house, I'd plant fruit."

"Fruit trees?"

"Is that where fruit grows?"

"Mostly."

"Peaches and pears?"

"They grow on trees, all right."

"That's what I'd plant."

"I guess I don't want a house because I don't want a yard."

"Where your kids gonna play?"

"In the park," she says. "Oh, who am I kidding? I'm not even married and we're talking about my kids."

"When did you know what you wanted to be?" I ask her.

"I don't know when it really clicked, but I know when it started. I really, really liked playing Monopoly. I always won. Had to, you know? And people always went for the obvious like Park Place. They underestimated properties like Baltic and the railroads."

She sets me up in a big white fluffy bed in a room she calls the guest room. There's even a little desk and chair in there for when I want to write down something.

"It's late. Let's get some sleep, OK?"

I'm glad for my dreadlocks because I don't have to worry about fooling with my hair, which will wake up looking the same as it looked when it went to sleep. Mama used to have us sleep in shower caps when we had cornrows. I think of what Mama is doing or not doing, and thinking of Mama turns me sad, so I look for something to read.

"Is this more on the Burger Factory?" I hold up a research report.

"It is. You want me to find you something else?"

"How 'bout you read me this?"

"Read it to you?"

"Yeah. Like a bedtime story."

She climbs into the bed and sits up beside me. She doesn't have any makeup on and she looks tired and young at the same time. She is not like other white people. She is not afraid to touch me and be beside me skin to skin. She clears her throat.

"A reading from the book of Burger Factory."

"Your hands look like turtle shells," I say.

"They're dry. They're always dry." She gets hand cream, puts it on, and then holds my hands between hers so that way I get the cream too. I think of Mama then. She quit touching me when Sashay died. She quit saying, *Hey, Cashay? How's it going in school?* She never said, *You look like you miss Sashay like I do.* I know I should miss Mama, but I don't. I wish I did miss her.

"How come—" I stop myself.

"I know. You want to know why I'm not married, right?"

I push up my shoulders. "I don't need to know nothing."

"I just haven't found the right man who can deal with me too."

"What about that guy at the Catholic center? The one you were painting with that day."

"Michael? I don't think he likes me. He can't even fake it."

She clears her throat again and starts to read. "'In 2005, the Burger Factory made significant inroads into the ten-billion-dollar fast food market. With seventy-two new locations, and an updated menu, the Burger Factory, our analysts predict, will have an increased market share, followed by . . .'"

And then I go away. All the way—I'm out of there. And for a while I'm into a fluffy dream where they serve hamburgers, as many as I can eat. I'm having myself a good sleep, the kind with jerks and an open mouth, the kind with happy eating dreams, but then when I'm finished eating I go out into the street, where I sleep in a cardboard box and all night I hear the El train clanking in the distance and it makes me sad, thinking about how it's moving and going somewheres and I'm not.

CHAPTER
11

Since I'm set up with Allison, I don't have to hide anymore and I can go back to school for pretend Chinese New Year. Ms. Feeley says that during the real Chinese New Year, which is in February, folks in China have a big cleanup, so she tells us we're doing it for spring and to get off our duffs and clean her classroom while she goes to the teachers' lounge to grade papers. We know for a fact that she will go outside for a smoke, then go into the lounge and brag about the multicultural extravaganza she's got going in her classroom.

Still, I don't get mad at Ms. Feeley, because she didn't get mad at me. We both know there's not much investment in aggravation. Not much return in disgust.

We all Zen out on Windex and bleach. I stop to read the paper and check my stock picks. Everything's going down, even technology. In the toilet, like Allison says. There's a story in there about a woman serial killer who was put to death. She says she'll be back, and she mentions some movie. Why do bad people always say they're coming back, and never the good people?

This morning, while Allison ran five miles—five miles!—on her treadmill, I spent a whole hour taking a bath in Allison's white bathtub, trying every different kind of flowery potion she has. Most of the bottles had *energize* written somewhere on them. It was hard to leave that bathroom, but Allison had dried my clothes warm, and after we dressed, she bought me a blueberry muffin and a chai tea and I ate and drank in the cab on the way to school. She told me it's what you do every day that changes you.

"We all have habits. Some are good, some are bad. A doctor once told me if I didn't run every day, I'd probably have some other habit, maybe even a bad drug habit. I just happened to pick a good habit. Think about what you do every day, and then ask yourself if it's good or bad. You can change your habits. Your habits can change you. Habits are your organizing principles."

While she drank coffee and talked into her cell phone about assets and telecom companies, I thought about what I do every day. Wash, eat, and go to school. Repeat. We drove through the financial district where men hustled into buildings that looked like giant toasters. Everyone was up, hurrying, carrying their paper coffees, and there I was, one of them. Now I knew I'd never want to just laze around the apartment in the morning, waiting for something to happen. These people were up and going, moving and shaking, making what they needed to happen happen.

When we passed a sign saying that the market was down, Allison groaned.

"That's how I measure my moods," she said, pointing to the sign. "Just when I think we're at the depth of the business cycle, something reminds me that there's always more room to go down." She punched numbers into her cell phone. "Get me Trading."

"Do you always think about the market?" I asked while she was on hold.

"Pretty much, yeah. The market's my life. Life is the market. What else is there?" She looked at me like she just remembered something. She smiled a nervous smile I had not seen on her before. "You know, love is a lot like the stock market. You save and save and you put yourself into it a little bit at a time and you hope for this tremendous return."

The phone was still stuck to her head when she told me to have a "terrific day" and she kissed me— kissed me!—on the cheek goodbye. I felt I had to say something back.

"Your hair fits on your head real good today," I said.

"Thank you, Cashay," she said, touching her hair. "That's so nice of you to say. I used a different blower." In the morning, before work, she had a warm, perfumy smell. Even after the cab drove away, I could smell her in the air all around me.

* * * *

Before I leave school, I stop by Ms. Feeley's desk to ask if she can write me a letter of recommendation for Benson's.

"That new magnet school in the Village?" she says,

laughing. I nod. She's sitting in her seat, eating from a box of frosted animal crackers, which she does not offer me. The coffee cup in front of her is marked with lipstick stains that date back to the first day of school.

"Cashay," she says, "I'm going to finish my snack first." She sits there chewing, thinking, and looking me up and down while I wait. My hands curl up into fists. I've never asked nobody for nothing and now I'm torn between wishing I never said those nasty words to her back when I beat up Jeremiah on Valentine's Day to wishing I said more nasty words. I hold my breath and then let my air out. In my mind I'm counting to ten, but I hear Allison's voice saying the numbers.

Ms. Feeley wipes the crumbs off her chest, then picks up a pen and a pad of paper. She has big old rusty hands. "Now, what is it you want me to say exactly?"

My fists unwad. I tell her what I want, word for word. I use all those words I've heard Sister Pigtails use—*self-motivated, self-learner, curious,* and *inspired*— and damned if Ms. Feeley doesn't take it all down.

Ms. Feeley. She's not all bad. She taught me how to use the Internet because she said cyberspace might just be the only way out of here. She makes a habit of telling us how hard it is to teach us. There are thirty kids in her class. Half of us can read. We use the bottoms of plastic soda bottles for petri dishes and history books that end with Nixon. And Ms. Feeley says we're the lucky ones because at least we got ourselves a regular teacher and not a substitute. At least she shows up.

I watch Ms. Feeley type my letter on a typewriter with a missing *d.* I watch because I don't want nothing to go wrong that doesn't have to go wrong. That's what Allison says. Whatever you can control, control. The rest you just have to let happen.

Ms. Feeley hands me the letter. It must be hard, watching us come and go, most of us not moving on at all, and all the while Ms. Feeley's stuck in this cold classroom, waiting for her cigarette break, thinking up words that don't have *d*'s in them.

"Good luck, Cashay," she says, and I think she means it and I thank her the way I've been taught.

CHAPTER 12

Now that school's out, I'm spending more time behind the cash register at the Burger Factory because most of the kids who work here don't know nothing about numbers or acting nice and the manager says at least I know how to fake it.

I know now why Allison works as hard as she does. Keeps your mind off your own self and your own sorry life.

Every now and then I go to Aunt Jo'Neisha's for a home-cooked meal. I spend the nights at Allison's until she can work out something she calls "more binding" with Linda the social worker. Allison talks to me about time as an investment. Seems like me and my problems take a lot of everybody's time. Who wants to invest in a company that is experiencing such a decline? I imagine she says in her mind, *That girl, Cashay, she's like having a kid and I don't want kids. That girl, Cashay, she has so many damned problems, she could be bad luck. That girl, Cashay, she's just too much work and I don't want her around no more.*

I still have questions, though. At work I look around at the dirty tables and I think about Mama in rehab. What if every day you're faced with a negative net worth?

* * * *

In the afternoons, after work, Allison and I go to my building to check the mail, our new habit. I swear the world stock market must be closing earlier these days because I can't imagine Allison leaving work early just for me.

One afternoon, on the one day Allison doesn't say "Any news yet from Benson's?" I reach into the box and pull out a note addressed to me. It's from Aunt Jo'Neisha. "Where you been?" she writes. "Come by. I got a new sofa and two big chairs since you came last! Come again soon! Love, Aunt Jo."

"Anything else?" Allison says.

Inside the box, there's an envelope from Benson's with my name on it.

"You open it," I say.

Allison shakes her head, and I shake mine. "Let's do it together."

We open it and she reads.

"Cashay, you scored a ninety-eight! That's amazing! You nailed that test!"

"Keep reading," I say, watching her face. Her smile is going fast into a frown the way she does.

"But. I don't get it. That's a terrific score. Oh, Cashay, I'm so sorry. I don't understand. You live here and that's such a great score, and they're not accepting you."

"That's OK," I say, like saying this will make it OK. And I'm thinking, *Well, now I don't have to get used to anything new. This really is my life. It's going to stay like this.* "I can go to Freemont and I can buy my own cell phone 'n' some nice clothes 'n' won't nobody mess with me."

Allison leans over to hug me. From her purse she takes out a package tied up with yellow ribbons.

"I've been waiting to give this to you." She gives it to me and I open it. It's a cell phone.

She punches a button and her number shows up on the little screen. She shows me how to dial and then how to send the call. She punches another button and it's 911. She says all I've got to do is press the one button in case of an emergency.

"But I didn't get in," I say, my eyes stinging. "You said if I get in you'd get me the cell phone."

Allison hugs me. "Honey. In my book, you're in, and I *always* get a high return on my investments."

I thank her and I put the cell phone in my pocket.

She squeezes me tight. "Come on," she says. "Let's go home."

I let her keep hugging me, and I let her take me with her again, but I stop once because I have to turn around and look up at my building this time. It is the last of the last to come down. I count the windows and locate our place, and I find our bedroom window. Our room. She's still got her hair in two twists tied and decorated with red beads and she's smiling big, waving at me from our bedroom window. I see her so clearly. It feels like that shot was never fired and that day never happened and she wasn't buried after all. She was just resting and now she's up again, right there, waving down at me from our bedroom window. Because we still have a secret. We're nothing like other girls.

I wave goodbye.

"What is it?" Allison says. "Who are you waving to?"

I don't say anything. How can I? In the cab I keep touching my cell phone, and I stare down at the little lit-up screen, knowing Allison's number is in there somewhere. Still, I can't help but wonder, *How will I get hold of Sashay?*

* * * *

One day in late June, just when the weather has gotten summer warm, I take an order from a woman and just as I hand her the change and say "Have a nice day," who do I see but T-Rex himself and two of his bad-ass boys.

"Yo, check out Miss Business. You a hard lady to keep track of," he says.

I'm looking around, but everybody's busy making burgers in the back. No one's in line behind T-Rex and his friends. He probably scared them all off.

"Can I take your order?"

"I'm thinkin' maybe you can." His friends laugh.

Mr. Stanley comes out from prep. Mr. Stanley's the manager.

"Cashay, everything all right?"

"Yes sir," T-Rex says. "This fine young sista just takin' our order."

Mr. Stanley nods and leaves.

"I ain't your sista."

T-Rex squints his eyes at me.

"That skinny white bitch that comes around. What you call her? Allison."

"She don't give me no money if that's what you're thinking."

"Yeah. But you can get it."

"I don't steal from her and I ain't gonna start."

"You won't have to."

Mr. Stanley comes back.

"I'm going to have to ask you boys to leave."

"Who you callin' 'boy'?" one of T-Rex's friends says.

"We ain't eat nothin' yet."

"Don't make me call the police."

T-Rex fixes his stare on me, and says: "Up to you what happens, sista."

Mr. Stanley stands beside me while we watch them turn around and leave.

"You OK?"

"Yeah," I say. "Can I make a call?"

I want to hear Allison's voice. I want to know she's OK. I want to warn her about T-Rex. I go to the back and use my cell phone. But the woman on the other end of the line says Allison's in a research meeting. I leave a message: I say, *Tell Allison don't come pick me up at work today. I'm working late. Tell her I'll take a cab to her place later.* Then I turn my cell phone off and go back to work.

I get off work late. I don't mind walking in the dark, because I know nobody can see me. I read somewhere about the night being like a cloak and I get that now, walking down the sidewalk.

I don't see the green car come sidling up beside me. T-Rex and his pals never moved this fast before, and when I feel a cigarette-smelling hand over my mouth, I think how much like a gun a car door slamming sounds like.

They know exactly where she lives, and they drive there now, knowing where to put the car so no one will see. All this time, they've been following me. All this time.

"Cashay? You and me, we goin' for a walk."

T-Rex tells me where he wants me to take him and

when I say no he shakes my shoulders and says, "You're gonna do like I say."

I got to get out. I walk in front of T-Rex, knowing he's got that gun in his pocket aimed at me. All along I'm praying for a bullet to come stop us both because I can't stand that I'm fixing to bring this T-Rex trouble into Allison's house.

"Miss Cashay," the doorman says, looking over T-Rex. "How are you this evening?"

T-Rex is looking like T-Rex except he's got his cap pulled down over his fire hair. He's wearing baggy pants and his looks don't belong here.

"I'm OK," I say. "This here's my friend," I say, pointing to T-Rex. This is the first time I've come here on my own, without Allison. I lead T-Rex to the elevator, knowing, hoping the doorman suspects something's wrong. "Allison knows we're coming."

Outside, one of T-Rex's boys is behind the wheel, waiting in the green car.

The elevator doors close. T-Rex doesn't say anything, and I take the chance to look at him. He looks nervous, maybe because he knows he doesn't fit in or maybe because he's not really sure what he's going to do next. This is when I see that T-Rex must not really have a plan at all, so it is up to me to come up with one of my own.

The elevator dings, and when Allison opens the door, T-Rex steps to the side and she doesn't see him. She just looks happy to see me.

"Cashay!" she says. I don't know why, but I'm glad she's wearing jeans and her "Race for the Cure" T-shirt. At least she *looks* tougher. "You've gotta leave your cell phone *on.* I've been trying to call you! I'm supposed to be looking after you, remember? Oh, forget about it—you're here now. I want you to meet Michael." She opens the door wider and I see a man I recognize from the center stand up in the living room. This Michael is coming toward me with his hand out. I'm shaking my head. "I got your message at the office. We've just come back from a movie."

T-Rex pushes me inside.

"Lady, just do like I say and nobody'll get hurt." T-Rex pulls the gun out of his pocket and Allison reaches out to me. Michael has both his hands up.

"Whoa. Steady," Michael says.

T-Rex lets go of my arm and holds his gun with two hands now. I can tell he's getting nervous. He hadn't thought of a Michael. "No, *you* steady, cowboy."

I stay quiet and I don't move. I want to scream out *I'm sorry sorry sorry for bringing this ugliness into your pretty life.*

"I don't want no trouble. I don't want to mess wit you. Just give me what you got."

Allison is not crying, but it looks to be that she could. She's talking, but I'm not listening. Then Michael starts talking. T-Rex is not looking at me. It's like it was at the hospital. It's like it is my whole life— I've gone invisible, only this time I don't mind. T-Rex only got stuff on his mind. He wants stuff, that's all he wants, more and more stuff. I say this to myself over and over as I slowly feel in my pocket for my cell phone. I find the right button by feel and turn the phone back on. I count the buttons. Speed dial is the thirteenth button and that's 911. I wait until T-Rex yells, and then I press down on the button. I start coughing when I think someone answers, and then I whisper Allison's address, hoping someone heard on the other end of the line.

We all four walk around the apartment like we're double-dating, except one of us has a gun. Allison gives him jewelry and watches and all the money in her purse. She gives over her wallet. Michael does the same. T-Rex puts it all in one of Allison's nice white pillowcases, one he gets from the bed in the guest room where I sleep.

When T-Rex has what he wants, he starts backing

out of the door. That's when he remembers me and he takes hold of my arm.

"Leave her here," Allison says.

"No. She comes with me," he says. "She don't belong here wit you."

In the elevator going down, T-Rex puts the gun back inside his pants. He looks through the stuff in the pillowcase like he's some kid looking through his Halloween candy. To him, a pillowcase full of stuff is the sum total of everything he wants. I don't think twice. I reach across and punch the stop button. The elevator jerks to a halt and we fall into each other, and while T-Rex hangs on to the guardrail with both hands, I grab hold of his gun. No alarm sounds. We just hang there. Me, holding that gun between both my hands, pointing it straight at T-Rex.

"Girl . . ." he starts.

"Don't you *girl* me."

"We can split it," he says, holding up the pillowcase. "Fifty-fifty."

If I shot him, right here and right now, it wouldn't matter. Not to me, anyway. I doubt I'd get into any real trouble. Self-defense. Who hasn't seen that show on TV?

His skin is black-blue and wet with sweat and his

eyes are tearing up. I shift my feet farther apart to hold my stance solid. I think of Sashay's eyes then, staring into mine when we were down there on the concrete together. I think of Mama staring up, seeing boys crawling on our living room ceiling. I think of my little baby brother's eyes closed and moist from screaming and crying all the time. Didn't all our misery start with this man here, T-Rex?

T-Rex's eyes make me sad and ashamed for him. All I see is fear and want. All he wants is his stuff and his life, but for what?

"Say it," I say. The words come out a whisper.

"What you want me to say?" he says, angry.

"You know," I say, louder now. "Say it."

He looks down, shaking his head. He touches the guardrail. "It was an accident," he says, slow and quiet-like. He looks up at me. "It was an accident." He can barely pronounce that word, *accident.* "I meant to shoot Big Buddha that first shot. But it got to Sashay. I didn't mean to."

"You're not even sorry. You shot my sister. You went and killed my baby sister. You messed up everything and now you're messing with the last good thing I got and you're not even sorry." And I'm crying. I'm sucking in air and I'm crying.

The gun hangs limp in my hands now. T-Rex pushes me aside, takes the gun from me, and then pulls the stop button out so that the elevator clunks and the buttons and numbers light up and we start going down again.

He raises his gun. "I ain't going to jail."

"Why don't you just say you're sorry?"

He opens his mouth.

The elevator dings just then and the number one lights up. The door opens, and when it does I hear, "Hold it right there!" Four Chicago policemen stand at the open doors in front of us, their guns all pointed at me and at T-Rex.

T-Rex drops his gun.

One policeman points to the cameras hanging from the elevator ceiling, telling me they got it all on film.

* * * *

A policeman has his hand on T-Rex's head while he puts T-Rex in the car. T-Rex is yelling, "I got no priors. You got nothin' on me."

I think of everything T-Rex has just said in the elevator and wonder if it amounts to a confession. Cuffed next to the policeman, T-Rex doesn't look big or tough anymore. He looks more like a kid, a punk. He says something that even makes the policeman look down, ashamed. T-Rex is nothing to anybody right now. He is nothing with nobody. You have to have pity on this. He looks at me. At first he squints, like he can't see. But then he looks past me, and then all around him like he's looking at this part of Chicago for the last time. He shrugs.

CHAPTER
13

At the Lincoln Park Zoo, the giraffes toss their heads up to the sky, then bend down to eat something from the ground, curving their necks into a letter C.

"She looks like she's stargazing," Michael says, pointing to one giraffe still looking skyward.

Allison reads us the sign. "Her name is Jennifer and she lost her mother last year."

I want to feed her something, but we're only allowed to feed the goats. I stay a while with Jennifer Giraffe, and I get used to that long blue tongue coming out of her mouth. I like the giraffes best with their big, wide-apart eyes and long lashes—you don't think about those parts on a giraffe.

"I wonder if she thinks about her," I say.

"Mother Nature is funny," Michael says. "She gave animals a certain amount of selfishness to survive and a little bit of compassion to make the survival worthwhile."

We pass the lions and Allison reads from the brochure that lions have a life span of only sixteen years. Michael looks at the one lion in his cage and he says, "I can't imagine how that would feel. To be in a jungle and look up and see that lion coming at you."

Allison and I just look at each other and roll our eyes. We're both thinking: *Been there.*

Pictures don't tell the whole story. Nothing really prepares you for the way things feel. When you're standing in front of a live lion, you remember you forget. You forget how really big and dangerous animals can be. You forget how nice they can be too. A lion still looks so much like a cat, but it's not. You forget how far he's come. You forget how far you've come.

It has been one October since Sashay died.

Already times and the economy have changed.

Linda Johnson, the social work lady, was there

outside Allison's building waiting for us one afternoon. We were going to have a meeting to discuss my
permanent situation.

We sat in Allison's living room and Linda said,
"Cashay. Last week, your mother's rights were termi-
nated for failure to protect. She's going to be in rehab
for some time." And then she talked about where I
was supposed to go, and she had it in her mind to put
me into a foster home, but she did some digging and
she's gone and found out that I do have a relative
nearby, and the state likes to put children with relatives, and it's my Aunt Jo'Neisha, who says she'd like
nothing better than to have me come live with her.

"But Cashay's already living with me," Allison said.

They both looked at me. "It's a nice place," I started.
"But it is a long ways off."

"But you can stay here, Cashay. For good."

Allison is just about the nicest lady I know. I want
to be with her, but I don't want to live with her. Her
life would change me into someone I know I am not.
That's just what I know I know.

"You got your dreams, and I got mine," I said, real
gentle-like.

And that's how I got to where I live now, with
Aunt Jo'Neisha in the Village.

* * * *

It was Allison's idea for me to reapply to Benson's. She thought I had a better chance, living in the Village and all, and she called Benson's herself, explaining to me the importance of what she calls "follow-up."

"You listen here," she said on her cell phone. She wasn't yelling. She was calm and steady. "This young lady scored a ninety-eight percent on that entrance exam. I know for a fact that no one scored higher. She *earned* a spot in that school. If Cashay Thomas is not enrolled at your school this fall I will alert both the *Tribune* and the *Sun-Times,* as well as the mayor's office." She told this person she was talking to her name again. She didn't say anything while she listened. Then she said, "I understand." And "I appreciate your concerns." And "Thank you." She pressed a button. She was pale and tired-looking. Her mascara was smudged.

"We'll need to go shopping," she said.

"What for?"

She sighed. "They wear uniforms at Benson's."

I smiled a big Sashay smile.

"How you know nobody else scored higher?"

She looked out the window, smiling too. "I don't."

Then my smile fell off my face. "But I wasn't good enough before, then you call and now I am? Maybe they don't want me there."

She turned and took both my hands in hers. "Look, Cashay. You earned this yourself. You earned that ninety-eight percent one hundred percent on your own. No one took that test for you."

I nodded. "But you had to call."

"Everyone needs a little push now and then. 'No man is an island.' That's John Donne, I think." She looked at me, and then started singing the corniest song I ever heard, nudging me to join in. And I did. And we sang. *"I get by with a little help from my friends. Oooo I'm gonna try with a little help from my friends."*

* * * *

Benson's is new. The floors feel springy and the air is lighter. I think the rooms must be farther apart and the ceilings higher. The walls are yellow. There are more white girls at my school, and with them come white-girl problems. One girl couldn't come to school because her pet iguana was having seizures.

And it's funny too. Not like in funny ha-ha, but like funny strange, because since I live in the Village and not in the projects, I can go to Benson's. But I don't get all mad and huffy about them taking me now and not then. No, sir. I keep my mouth shut, write what I need and want to say in my red hostility log, and then go off to that big new shiny school.

Allison comes over to Aunt Jo'Neisha's to help me with my homework, and when she first saw me in my new blue uniform, my dreadlocks down to the pockets on my shirt, she said, "Cashay! You're so pretty." I was wearing what they call loafers even though I'm no loafer. I'd taken off my old Sashay shoes. They had turned a shade lighter than light brown, and I put them under my bed next to the shoebox with the cicada shells.

"You don't have to sound so surprised," I said to Allison. "You *could* try faking it."

Allison helps me with my Algebra II Honors.

"You look confused," she says at the start.

"I'm not confused," I say. "Not in a bad way."

She smiles and says, "Well, at last you're being *challenged.*"

She teaches me new formulas and more. When she sips coffee, she sighs and says, "Oh." When she opens a newspaper, she snaps it open like it's a best-selling romance novel she just has to get to, and she says, "Well, now, let's see what the market's up to today."

When she eats, it's never just fine, it's always delicious. She says, "Isn't this delicious, Cashay? Isn't this the most wonderful bread you've ever tasted?" I say, "Yeah, I guess so." And then once I say this, the bread really does taste better, and more like cake.

I tell her she's not like other women. She tells me I'm not like other teenagers. We work, but we're not working like other people who work for food or for drugs or for clothes or for rent. We're working for something more. We're working for happiness, for fineness, for something more than OK. Who knew that these were things you could work for?

"I love you," I say to Allison one day, out of the clear blue.

"Oh, Cashay," she says. "Thank you."

"Don't thank me. I didn't do it. It just happened by its own self."

* * * *

I still have a lot to figure out, stuff that doesn't have anything to do with numbers or the economy. Stuff like why your tongue likes to rest on the roof of your mouth and whether or not Mama will ever get better in rehab, and if I'll see her full-time again.

I visit her one time. Aunt Jo'Neisha takes the train

with me to a white building that looks like a grammar school with a nice lawn. In the hall, we pass a woman yelling at someone to turn off the electric fan even though there is no fan. She asks Aunt Jo'Neisha if she could swallow a fan. Jo'Neisha does her *umn umn umn*, takes my arm, and walks on.

Mama has some meat on her bones now and she looks at me like she's seeing me for the first time. After she hugs us both, she sits down and smokes and smokes cigarettes, one after another. We all three talk small talk until finally I ask what no one's asking. I ask after my baby brother. Mama looks at me, trying to be real calm, but I see her hands shaking as she lights up another cigarette. She goes on about Mr. Giggles and how they took him to another facility outside the state, in Indiana of all places, and I'm thinking, *Good. That's the end of him.*

She says she signed the papers too. What papers? I say. The papers, she says. She has a leftover voice, like she screamed out all but what's left.

"His foster family wanted to adopt him and I let them. Those papers. Adoption papers."

"Can I go visit him?"

"No," she says, and that is it. Over and out.

Mama can't help but look nervous to see me and

Aunt Jo'Neisha, like we are ghosts from the past she doesn't want to think about much anymore. Maybe she'll come around. When she gets better and quits shaking.

When we leave, I watch Aunt Jo'Neisha and Mama hug. Some people are better huggers than others. Aunt Jo'Neisha is in the top 2 percent. She once told me that when you hurt to just hold on and the pain will eventually go away. Me? I'm still holding on.

I hear Mama whisper "Thank you" to Aunt Jo'Neisha. Mama's shoulders shake like she might be crying and she holds on tighter.

Aunt Jo'Neisha, she says, "You take care of yourself, baby sister. You're the only sister I have."

I swallow hard.

Jo'Neisha and Mama are the exact polar opposites. I have to wonder, Were they ever close? But watching them, anyone can see they are sisters. That never goes away.

Later, when Allison and I go visit the afterschool center for a reunion, I take Sister Pigtails aside and ask her about how I can best advise my mother. I ask, What if she meets another man like Mr. Giggles at rehab? I say, "Shouldn't she be on some kind of birth control?" Sister gets all nervous and tells me maybe a daughter shouldn't discuss such things with her mother or anybody else. Sister Pigtails is all right, but her after-school center closes because of budget cuts.

Last year, after a year of mentoring, Sister Pam left the sisterhood and adopted Juanita. Juanita says that Sister Pam is not bad to live with. She says she can be pretty fun to be around when she's not mad. I guess I can understand that.

* * * *

This fall the sky doesn't go straight to dark. It goes from blue to pink to gray. The weather hasn't turned really cold yet, and you can still take a walk after dinner or even go get a movie to rent if you have all the right equipment. Aunt Jo'Neisha doesn't have a TV. She likes radio and she's doing all right. She got a 5-percent raise plus medical and she started taking classes to become a nurse's aide.

"We need to start a nest egg," I tell her one night before she goes to work at the hospital. "We need a reserve. We need to save for our future."

She pulls her jacket on and hugs me tight. "Where do you come up with this?" she says. *Umn umn umn.*

I tell her the truth. I tell her what I know. We have a lot of challenges: a roller-coaster market, economic uncertainties, eroding consumer confidence. But we can deal. I pack our lunches every day to save money. I like to wrap our sandwiches in foil for a nice tight fit. You can get a five-pack of foil at the Dollar Store.

When Aunt Jo'Neisha bites into one of my fine sandwiches she says she tells anybody around, "Lord, that girl can pack a sandwich!" and "I sure wish I'd gotten Cashay sooner."

I know what she means, but I don't have the heart to say, *No, Aunt Jo'Neisha. I'm glad for those years with Mama and Sashay even though thinking about them can turn me so sad.* Aunt Jo'Neisha says *she's* glad we've both let go of the big crying.

I still write in my hostility log.

HOSTILITY LOG ENTRY #197

WHEN: Friday, after algebra homework.
SCENE: Allison says *sashay* can be a word for the special way you walk. It comes from the French word *chasse*, which is a dance step. I say couldn't it also be part of the word *satchel*? Like what you use to carry stuff? Allison asks me to tell her more about Sashay. I tell her.

Sashay. She was spacey. Out there, you know? She could have been an artist, but she didn't paint. She just acted the way people say artists act. People say she laughed too much. She was too happy to be living around here. People thought she was *special* like retarded special because she was always smiling. We were sisters, you know? Sisters. If we had played tennis, we would have been like Venus and Serena except Sashay would have never beat me and I would have never beat her. We would have just played. On and on like that.

The thing is we knew what we had. We knew. Sashay and me. We both knew. When she died, it was worse than terrible because I knew that we both knew how good we had it. Now I'm glad we both knew so it's not as terrible anymore.

Back when Sashay's death was still new, I felt like my arm had been cut off. My right arm. If a lizard loses its tail, another one grows back in its place. It's not like my arm grew back or nothing. It's more like I got my balance back with the one arm, so that I could learn to walk around, jump, even, without leaning too far off to one side. Now I feel a lot like that lizard with the regrown tail.

I still think about Sashay sleeping with all the other sleeping dead. Maybe somebody somewhere up in the sky is taking care of Sashay. Maybe. Sometimes I'm sure she's still around, hiding somewhere behind my ribs, under my tongue, or maybe even inside my ear. I can feel her around me, watching me, and I like that. I even sometimes think, *Hey, you see that, Sashay?*

Aunt Jo'Neisha lets me keep Sashay's box of cicadas under my bed next to my old shoes. I keep the box, not because it makes me sad, but because it makes me happy, remembering.

FEELING: This feeling I have for Sashay isn't just love. Love is something somebody made up a long time ago. No. This thing is so real I could be knocking against it, hard, and it wouldn't break. It's pepperminty and icy and clear as glass, but it curves around me, warm like a fuzzy shield. It's there when I wake up and it's there when I go to sleep. Just like Sashay was. Like Allison said, you don't have to be dead *and* gone.

THOUGHT: People who smile that much shouldn't be the ones to die. Still, I think about the last thing Sashay said to me. She said, "Don't be mad."

ACTION: Finish my homework and make my bed. Cook for Aunt Jo'Neisha and get to school and to work on time.

INVOLVEMENT: High.

* * * *

Sometimes, during the week, I meet Allison and Michael uptown for lunch in the financial district. They're engaged now and they've got a wedding planned for Christmas. Allison asked me to be her maid of honor, and even though I know I will probably have to squeeze into some uncomfortable, scratchy dress, I can't stop smiling.

I always have plenty to talk about over lunch. I keep reading the newspaper. Every morning. People at the Burger Factory leave them behind at the tables. Even when the news is bad, reading the paper and knowing what's happening outside of where I live now makes me feel like I'm alive in the world. Knowing things, even if they happen in Costa Rica, makes me feel alive, like I'm a person who *should* know and think about such things, like I'm a person who cares.

One Friday, we three meet up at a diner close to Allison's office.

"You're orange," I say.

"Oh. That," Allison says. "I tried a new kind of tanning cream. You should see me in these wedding dresses! I look terrible in white if I'm not tan. It's not that bad, is it?"

"You're *orange,*" I say again.

Already Michael's laughing.

The three of us have our say about what all is wrong with people and the world and we talk ourselves hungry. I ask them, have they ever noticed how some people think women can't earn a ton of money because they don't think women know how to be mean and aggressive? Allison and Michael exchange looks and Allison says, "Boy, are they ever wrong!"

When they bring out Allison's fruit and Michael's coffee and my pie I give Allison what I came to give her.

"I read that some maids of honor give the bride a present. I've been working and saving up," I tell her. "This is for you." I hand over the box and she opens it right away just like I would.

"Oh, Cashay." She lifts up the necklace. It's got some letters on a gold charm and she looks and reads it. "'Allison.'" Michael puts it on for her and she kisses me. It looks to me she likes it. "Thank you so much, sweetie," she says. "But you've got it all wrong."

I look at the necklace to make sure her name is spelled right.

"The bride is supposed to give the maid of honor the gift." She gives me a box and inside is a framed picture of the two of us standing in front of the giant heart at the Museum of Science and Industry. I'm bolt upright, stiff as a board, and Allison has her hand on my shoulder. We're standing together. Close. Inside the box is another, smaller box with a gold necklace with a heart-shaped pendant, and inside the pendant is my name: Cashay.

"Listen, Cashay," Allison says, putting the necklace on me. "I want you to know that you can come over for a sleepover anytime you want. Before and after Michael and I are married. I mean that."

When we're finished with dessert, Allison and Michael sneak a kiss goodbye. To her he looks fine. To her he's got some serious mojo. But all I can see are the comb marks in his hair. After he leaves for his office, Allison and I stand for a while under the stock meter. Here is where she'll go her way and I'll go mine. Just for today. Everyone around us is in a hurry. I can see their shoulders coming at me, their heads down and into a cell phone. There is some warm in the air. We watch a black man going after his girlfriend, and they kiss there on the corner in front of the world to see. Sirens wail.

Allison looks up at the meter reader. What did she say to me once? The meter measures her mood. While we were eating our lunch, the market went down and the decline still isn't over. Allison just smiles and touches her necklace.

"I'm really, really happy right now," she says.

"So am I," I say, tucking our picture under my arm, making sure my necklace stays outside my T-shirt. I have to swallow. It's not supposed to be like this. Feeling good like this is not supposed to feel as real and as red as when Sashay died. I wish I could give Sashay some of this happiness I have right now.

I am very sure that everything is going to be all right. Sure, sometimes I feel like I'm walking outside in the dark and I don't know where I'm heading, and I know that the world is not going to stop for me or for anyone else. Somebody else will shoot somebody's sister and maybe get away with it. Maybe not. The market will go up and then it will go back down again. But the ups and downs don't seem as exhausting as they once were. I'm game now. I'm ready to be a player—not a gambler, but someone who does her research, someone with a plan. Someone with serious interest.

ACKNOWLEDGMENTS

My thanks to Rob Griffith, Arion Johnson, Johanna Hemminger, Jo'Neesha, Bosse High School, Jasmine Lee, Adam and Brian Ernsting, Paul Bone and his copyediting class, Jim Ellerbrook, Joy Van Meerveld, Reba and Mathew McMellon, and Jack Haseman for loving to read, Eilidh for being born so I could tell Tamara Wandell about Cashay, Dr. Jeana Lee and Jessica MacLeod for help with medical questions, and all the teachers, mentors, and children at Patchwork Central for their research assistance. My thanks to William Blair & Company and the Chicago Stock Exchange for allowing me to research the stock market and the investment business. My thanks to the Museum of Science and Industry, Chicago's Lincoln Park Zoo, the University of Evansville, Mr. and Mrs. John Dunn, the Southwestern Indiana Arts Council, Evelyn Walker and the Evansville/Vanderburgh County libraries, Evansville, Indiana's Literacy Council, the New Harmony Project, the Women's Fund, the Mississippi Library Association, Pass Christian Books, and Ann Abadie and the Mississippi Institute of Arts and Letters for being socially responsible and for their ongoing literary interest and support. And my thanks always to my wonderful husband and son, Pat and James O'Connor, our dog, Samantha, my agent, Jennie Dunham, my editor, Margaret Raymo, and publicist Karen Walsh at Houghton Mifflin for everything.